BROOKS

LYNKS AT TRYST FALLS
BOOK 3

BROOKLYN BAILEY

Copyright © 2023 Brooklyn Bailey
All rights reserved.

Lynks at Tryst Falls is a work of fiction. Names, characters, and incidents are all products of the authors imagination and are used fictitiously. Any resemblance to actual events or persons, living or dead, is entirely coincidental.

Any trademarks, service marks, product names, or named features are assumed to be the property of their respective owners and are used only for reference. There is no implied endorsement.

Brooks Paperback: 978-1-959199-40-3
Brooks eBook: 978-1-959199-39-7

Cover by @Germancreativ on Fiverr

❀ Created with Vellum

DEDICATION

In February 2023, the world lost a beacon of light, strength, and positivity. I dedicate this book to my best friend Dawn Holt. She fought 8 long years with Stage IV Colon Cancer and chemotherapy every other week. Even during her 8-year battle, her smile and sunny personality got me through each day. She inspired me to be a better person, to spread happiness, and to share positivity even when I'm feeling a bit down.

DEDICATION

To Enhance Your Reading:
Check out the **Trivia Page** at the end of the book
before reading Chapter #1.
No Spoilers—I promise.

Look at my Pinterest Boards for my inspirations for characters,
recipes, and settings. (Link on following pages.)

Prefer your romance on the **steamier** side?
Look for this story under my **Rated R** author name Haley Rhoades.
HaleyRhoades.com

1
HE'S FREAKING HERE!

Brooks

"Hey, guys," I greet the gym rat and straight-laced man as they enter my tattoo parlor on Thursday in early June. "Looking to get inked today?" I ask as they scan the walls and approach me at the counter.

"I am bringing you a newbie," I-love-lifting-weights-and-chugging-protein-shakes guy announces proudly.

Called it. I knew the guy in the button-down shirt was uptight. *He probably wants a tattoo honoring his mom.*

"Any idea what and where you want it?" I inquire, dreading his answer.

"I am looking for something even my t-shirt will cover," he explains.

Under a t-shirt. So, he plans to hide it 24/7.

"I am warring with two quotes by Nietzsche," he states.

Whoa! I did not see that coming. Maybe I judged these two guys too quickly.

"I am Brooks, by the way." I wave awkwardly.

"I'm Ryan, and he's Maddux," the taller and wider one says.

"So, Maddux, why a tattoo? And why today?" I sound nosey, but getting the inaugural tattoo is a major step, especially for a straight-laced guy like him. I need my customers to be happy when they leave my parlor, not spreading negative experiences.

"He's talked about finally getting a tattoo for two years now," Ryan states.

"Bro, I can answer for myself," Maddux chides.

My thoughts focus on the word "bro," wondering if these two are really brothers. They are both tall—over six feet—and have blonde hair, although it's styled differently. Ryan wears his blonde curls ear-length and tousled for that just-crawled-out-of-bed look. Maddux trims his short on the sides with about two inches of product-tamed, perfectly styled, wavy curls on top. Their matching blue eyes, sexy smiles, and dimples lead me to believe they are, indeed, brothers.

"I need an artist's help with the design. I want more than a quote. I'd like it inside a tribal band or a tribal sun tattoo. I'm open to a thigh tattoo if we choose a larger design."

I like that. I love designing unique pieces. I get to show my creativity on paper as well as on the body. I tug my sketchpad from under the counter, opening to the first clean page. In the top corner, I write "M-a-d-d-o-x."

"It is 'u-x' not 'o-x,'" he immediately corrects.

I fight the urge to roll my eyes. *It is my sketch, not a government form. Chill, dude.*

"What are the two quotes?"

Maddux's tongue darts out to wet his overly-plump lower lip, his teeth dragging over it in contemplation. I am momentarily distracted by his mouth.

"My first choice is, 'No artist tolerates reality.'"

My eyes fly to the purple bumper sticker hanging halfway up the wall to my right with the same quote in black lettering. I first read the line in high school and have kept it near me ever since. I place the quote on the page under his name, along with the second, longer quote: "Without music, life would be a mistake."

Hmm... I love both of them.

"Do you have photos of the artwork you like without the quotes?" I ask.

Maddux shakes his head. "I like the sun because it is a symbol of strength and protection. Let's go for it and design a Polynesian thigh tattoo; include a sun and that quote."

I attempt to pull my arms from the counter as he points to the reality quote. I'm not quick enough. His fingers skim over my forearm. I freeze, awaiting a jolt that…does not come. *Odd.* Even the slightest touch, especially with a stranger, brings on visions. I open my eyes, looking up at the tall, blonde hunk, who is looking down at me with concern. His sky-blue eyes ping-pong between mine.

"I'm sorry if I scared you," he murmurs, tucking his hands into his pockets.

Biting my lips, I nod then return my gloved hands to the sketchpad. As I sketch a thigh, I attempt to decipher what happened a moment ago. I always see the future when a stranger touches me. I did not imagine his fingertips grazing my arm. I can still feel the heat where he made contact. I've found fingers hold the longest, most vivid visions. Sometimes, I block them out, but only when I focus really hard. Even then, it's only with family and my close, close friends. I spare a glance up at the two men before I place a sunburst on the thigh then design repeating patterns around it.

"Usually, a band tattoo symbolizes rebirth or that life continues," I explain. "The arm bands often commemorate a death. Is there anything or anyone in your life you would like to include in the design?" I pause my pencil, looking only at Maddux.

He looks at Ryan for a long moment before his striking blue eyes return to me. "I had cancer when I was four." He shrugs nervously. "I do not want a long band of ribbons; I do not want pity."

"Oh, I would not do that," I vow. "Are you still…"

He shakes his head, answering my unspoken question. "I'm in remission and have been for over 20 years now."

Ryan knocks three times on my wooden countertop.

Maddux smiles, and I am lost in the faint lines at the sides of his mouth, the parenthesis at the edge of his cheeks, and the crinkles at the corners of his eyes. *He really is a marvelous specimen of a man.* I long to sketch his face. Instead, I attempt to burn it into my memory to draw later when I am alone.

"Let me play around with this," I say, my pencil once again sketching. "I will hide a cancer ribbon within the design. Discreet but a celebration of the life you've lived."

"Thank you," he says, his voice further hypnotizing me.

He places his palm on top of my left wrist on the counter. I fight my instinct to pull away, welcoming visions of his future. *I need to figure out how his first touch produced no images.* I stare at his hand as it touches me. *Still no visions. Maybe I'm sick. This has never happened before.* I look up at this neat-as-a-pin, perfectly-put-together man, marveling that he's blocking my gift. *Perhaps he has a gift like mine.*

"I will spend a day or two on the design. You can call the shop after that, and we will set up a time for you to come and approve it."

Maddux nods.

In a final attempt to figure this all out, I remove my glove, extending my hand to shake his. *Nothing. Even if he had no future, I'd see his death.* Instead, I receive no visions. Next, I shake body-builder Ryan's hand.

Mistake. Big mistake. Vision after vision swarms my head. Not just one event. Many. I see tomorrow, next week, next month, next year, and beyond. There are so many visions that I nearly faint before I withdraw my hand, waving them away.

I stare at the glass door long after they leave, not seeing the city square beyond. Of all the tattoo parlors, they chose mine. In all the visions Christy, Harper, and Ry gave me, I never, ever saw this event.

Life as we know it is over, and Christy doesn't even have a clue. What's worse, she won't allow me to alert her.

Ryan Freaking Harper is here!

2

I CAN'T SEE

Brooks

My next two appointments pass with my thoughts on my failure to see visions with this potential client, Maddux. With each passing hour, I grow more frustrated. This devastatingly handsome man befuddles me. I am equal parts attracted to him and pissed that he has the power to block visions from me.

I doubt I will ever hear from Maddux again. His discomfort in my parlor leads me to believe he will remain an ink virgin.

My cell phone vibrates in my back pocket.

CHRISTY
We're home

I glance at the wall clock to the right of the front counter. It's 4:30. *Miguel should arrive for his shift by five. Christy knows I will work until about six, so dinner will be ready at 6:30.* I open my sketch pad. On instinct, my fingers grasp a pencil, rapidly shading my fantasy of

Maddux's muscular thigh before adorning it with two possible designs.

"Brooks!" Miguel shouts, pulling me from my imagination. He chuckles when I startle. "Your phone keeps vibrating." He points to the counter beside me.

> CHRISTY
> dinner 15 min

I note the time is now 6:25. I blink rapidly, unsure how two hours pass without my notice.

> ME
> (thumbs up emoji)

I close my sketchpad, clutching it to my chest, and walk from area to area. I shut down everything except the front register and Miguel's area. A few minutes later, I'm climbing the steps to my apartment.

Quietly walking through the door, I find five-year-olds Harper and Ry giggling in their seats with their backs to me at the table. Their long, blonde curls are wet from a recent bath, and they wear the *Nightmare Before Christmas* pajamas I bought for them.

"Where is Miss Brooks?" Harper asks.

"I am right here," I announce, entering the kitchen as Christy pulls the baking dish from the oven.

"Go sit," I instruct, my tone bitchy. "I will carry this to the table." I cringe. *I shouldn't let my day spill over onto my roommates.*

"Bad day?" Christy dares to ask as I take my seat.

I bite my lips tightly between my teeth as I nod.

"Wanna talk about it?" she offers as she scoops rice onto each little girl's plate.

"I can't," I bite.

Christy balks at my response. *I did it again.* In my struggle to process my lack of visions, I'm taking my frustration out of my best friend.

"I want to tell you, but I can't," I state flatly between bites.

Christy focuses on the girls, cutting chicken into bite-sized pieces for them. After hours at the swimming pool while Christy worked, Harper and Ry struggle to keep their eyes open as they eat. My mind reels with causes for my reaction to Maddux's touch, which keeps me from chatting. Christy opts not to fill the void. Rather, she occasionally glances in my direction. Our dinners are never this quiet.

"I guess I can share part of it," I offer. "A new guy and his brother…" I glance up at Christy's worried face then back to my food.

"Well…he wants his first tattoo. While I was sketching, he touched me."

She gasps, thinking this is what's upset me; she thinks I experienced a vision that scared me.

"Actually, he touched me three times," I inform.

Christy chokes on her food, coughing and sputtering for a moment. I'm careful, uber careful, to avoid touching everyone, even her girls. I wear gloves at all times in my shop. I use them as a protective barrier for me more than for my customers. I learned long ago that two pairs of latex gloves prevent most visions when I create their tattoos. On rare occasions, a stranger will catch me off guard by touching me.

"Tell me," she urges. "Tell me about the visions so I can help you work through them."

I shake my head. I've shared some pretty screwed up and freaky visions with her. *She'll think it must be bad if I won't tell her in front of the twins.*

"Girls, go brush your teeth and get ready for bed," Christy instructs, anxious to hear my story.

We watch two sleepy kids slide from their chairs and trudge to the hallway. Little ears now gone, Christy looks to me for an explanation. Again, I shake my head. She prepares to demand to hear about the visions, but I silence her, raising my hand between us.

"He touched me three times, and I had no visions. None." I look for her reaction.

"No visions?" Christy murmurs, concerned about what this means. "Were you blocking him?"

I shake my head. "At the first touch, his fingers accidentally grazed my forearm as he pointed at my sketch."

"No visions?" she asks.

Again, I shake my head. "He perplexed me," I admit. "A million thoughts flooded to mind as I continued to sketch, so I was not focused when he placed his hand on my wrist."

My friend's eyes grow wide.

"Part of his hand met my wrist, and nothing." I pause, grinding my teeth. "I began to worry I was sick. So, I removed my glove to shake his hand goodbye, and still, no visions," I huff, frustrated with the entire situation. "To be sure I was not broken, I shook hands with his brother, and…"

Christy can't help but finish. "You had a vision."

"I had the most vivid, fast playing flashes I've ever experienced. Like, ten visions all in a minute's time. It made me light-headed," I confess.

"So, your gift is still intact. What does this mean?"

I stare at her, wishing she knew the future I saw, then I shake off that train of thought. She is serious in her desire not to know any visions involving her and the twins.

"I am not sure why I didn't have visions when Mad—he touched me," I state, afraid his name would clue her in on the vision. "Maybe he was blocking me." I shrug.

"You should ask him; maybe he could teach you to do it," Christy encourages.

"And how would that go?" I scoff. "So, I have visions with everyone but you. Do you have a gift, and if so, can you teach me to block visions like you do?"

She picks up the sarcasm I lay down.

"I can't tell strangers I have a gift. Word will get around, and I will lose clients."

She purses her lips at my dilemma.

"Tell me about the visions his brother gave you." Christy attempts to change the topic.

I shake my head, leaving no doubt this is not up for discussion.

There are only two types of visions I will not share: visions involving Christy and the twins—which she requested I keep to myself—and those that are heinous. As a mom, she claims she can't hear those, or she will never leave the house with her daughters.

"You should read to the girls tonight," she suggests, hoping their sweetness will help clear my mind.

Together, we make quick work of clearing the table. Christy offers to wash the dishes while I join the twins.

I don't read; instead, I quiz the girls for information.

"Who is this player?" I ask, pretending not to know the name of the gym rat that entered my parlor today.

The twins groan in unison.

"Ryan Harper," Ry states, frustration heavy in her voice. "We have his jersey."

I hear the unspoken "duh" in her tone.

"We told you a gazillion times; he's our favorite player," Harper adds.

"He's the one your mom cheers for?" I continue.

"He's her favorite player!" they announce.

Hmm... I really need to pay more attention when they watch football games. Not into sports, I lose myself in a book rather than cheer like the three of them do each week. I stare at the football posters on the twins' wall.

"He runs fast." Ry runs around the room as a demonstration.

"And he always catches the football," Harper brags, tossing her little Cardinals football and catching it.

"What's going on in here?" Christy asks, leaning against the bedroom door frame.

Both girls point to me. "She asked," they defend in unison.

"To bed, both of you," Christy orders, and they assume their spots on their pillows in the twin beds against the right wall.

I don't move. I continue to stare at the poster, studying every feature of the NFL player that is Ryan Harper.

"Brooks, is everything alright?" my friend asks.

"Everything is perfect," I lie with conviction.

Not believing me, Christy continues watching me closely.

When I bend down, closing my eyes to kiss Harper's hand then cheek, I hear Christy gasp from the doorway. I ignore her reaction, focusing on the visions flooding my mind.

Ryan Harper with Ry and Harper. They're at the club. Next, Christy joins the three of them at his house. I move to kiss Ry's hand and cheek. *Ry's hurt. Ryan drives them to the doctor; she wears a cast. The four of them are together at their wedding and on the field at his home games.* I draw in a deep breath of relief as I open my eyes and stand.

Like the visions Ryan shared with me this afternoon, the twins are happy, healthy, and thriving with their father in their lives. Christy is, too. I needed their touch and their visions to reassure me. Ryan's visions excited me, but I worried for my friend at the same time. The twins' viewpoints assure me. *Our lives are about to change—quickly and for the better.*

I walk towards Christy in the doorway. Her scrutiny weighs me down. It doesn't escape her that I purposely touched the girls and experienced visions. She smiles at her daughters and turns off the light.

Back in the kitchen, I pour two glasses of our favorite rosé, sliding one stemless wine glass across the butcher-block countertop to her.

"Let's talk," she urges.

We exchange a look.

"Explain," she instructs.

I shake my head, lips tight between my teeth.

"Brooks, it is clear the visions today upset you." Her eyes beg me to open up. "You kissed the girls; you were seeing their futures. What is up?"

I shake my head.

"Who were these guys, asking for a tattoo today?"

More head shaking.

"Brooks, help me understand," Christy pleads.

"They were good visions," I state, leaving her curious.

"The girls?"

I shake my head. "The guy at the shop. So many happy times, events, and a long, happy life."

"So, why are you so sullen?" she probes.

"I am not sullen. I am restrained." I smirk. "You ordered me not to share any visions I see for you and the girls."

With no more detail, I mime zipping my lips and locking them then tossing the key over my left shoulder. This is not the first time this has come back to bite her on the butt. Part of Christy wants to know everything I experienced today, even with the twins. Although she believes my visions and has witnessed them come true, she doesn't like knowing what lies ahead. She detests waiting around for the scene I saw to unveil itself. She becomes anxious, looking everywhere for it to happen. She stands firm and doesn't give me permission to tell her what I saw for Harper and Ry's future.

"I love our lives," I reassure, smiling before sipping my wine.

"No hints. You know the rules," she warns, shaking her finger at me.

"I am calling it a night," I state. "We have a big day tomorrow." I smirk, dropping another little hint there. I wave over my shoulder, taking my wine with me.

3

HE'S A RUNNER

Brooks

My fingers grip the pencil as my hand moves rapidly over the sketchpad. Before me, I attempt to recreate the magnificent male that happened into my parlor today.

I sketch Maddux head to toe with his almost-twin brother, Ryan, behind him. I recall the contrast of strength and power in their two forms. Ryan oozes brute strength; Maddux exudes business power.

In my sketch, I bring to life my imagination's idea of Maddux's defined chest, arms, abs, and thighs. Judging by the sight of his face, hands, and neck, I assume his skin to be golden, tanned by the sun.

Sculpted by yard work.
Wait. Swimming?
Hmm... Maddux in a swimsuit. Yum, yum.
But no. Running?
Yes. Running.
Maddux seems like a runner with long and lean muscles from head to toe. Long, powerful, corded muscles. Hard to my soft, pressing me into the mattress.
What the hell?

I brush off fantasies of my new client. *Where the hell did they come from?* I'm behaving like a teenager with her first crush instead of the 23-year-old woman I am. *I don't lust after a man I only met today.* I only fantasize about Hollywood Stars, not men near me.

Even if it were possible, Maddux is off limits. His brother belongs to my best friend, Christy. Well, he will by the weekend when they bump into each other again. Even if I could, it would not be wise to allow myself to be with Ryan's brother. I've seen their future; Ryan and Christy will be together forever.

I roll myself out of my bed, padding my way to the kitchen with my empty wine glass in hand. It's dark but for the nightlight in the kitchen and the glow of Christy's eReader screen on the sofa. *By going to my bedroom after dinner, I left her alone for the evening.*

"Hey," she calls, raising her head from her pillow.

"Want a refill?" I ask, wine bottle in hand.

She places her eReader on the cushion and joins me in the kitchen, placing her glass near mine. I note the level of wine in the bottle is lower than when I last poured. As it is not empty, I know she's only had one glass while I hid in my bedroom this evening.

"You seem in better spirits," Christy states, nudging her shoulder to mine. "What were you sketching?"

She knows me so well.

"Working on a new tattoo design," I state. *It's not really a lie.* I started by sketching possible designs for Maddux's thigh tattoo before I became distracted, imagining other parts of him.

"Clearing your mind." She thinks out loud.

I wish, I think to myself. My sketching stirred up more confusing feelings within me rather than clearing my head.

Brooks

The next three days fly by as my visions play out for Christy and her daughters. She bumps into Ryan at the club where she works, Ry breaks her arm, and Ryan swoops in to help. Christy and Ryan discuss the past, the present, and their daughters, and finally, today, the twins learned that their favorite NFL player, Ryan Harper, is their father.

Meanwhile, I've tried to process my lack of visions with Ryan's brother, Maddux. My mentor, Madam Alomar, assures me my gift is still intact and that he is precognitive immune. *He confounds me.* He is not at all my type, yet I cannot think of anything but him. Maddux haunts my thoughts all day and my dreams all night. I've tried music, wine, losing myself in my art—nothing erases his looks or his touch.

Slipping through the front door after a long day of tattoos, I'm greeted by the sounds of the girls all the way from their bedroom down the hall.

"Brooks!" the twins scream with glee.

Closing the door, I enter our alarm code. The sounds of little feet trotting up the hallway drown out the beeps of my fingers on the keypad.

"Brooks, Daddy is here!" Ry cheers. "Come see Daddy."

The girls run to Ryan's side, each taking a hand.

"See?" Ry points. "He's our daddy!"

Ryan nods his chin in that purely masculine guy way, with what I'm sure is his signature panty-melting smile greeting me.

"Hi again." I awkwardly wave.

"Hello. I'm Ryan Harper."

"She knows," Christy bites. "She could have given me a heads up," she says through gritted teeth.

"But *someone* has a pesky rule about me sharing those things," I quip.

Remembering Ryan is in the room, I look in his direction. I find his brow furrows at our talking in code.

"Sounds like the two of you share your own language just like the twins do," he chuckles.

"Back to bed," Christy orders, frustrated. "For the third time." She looks at me, hoping I get her meaning.

"Daddy has a brother," Ry tells me.

"And a mom and dad," Harper adds.

I smile, happy to witness their excitement. "I will leave you to this,"

I say, swirling my finger toward the twins now back in their bedroom with Ryan.

"Eyes closed," Ryan says as I exit the room. Beelining for wine, I am still able to hear their conversation in our little two-bedroom apartment.

"My brother Maddux is four years older than me. His house is by my house. He is your uncle, so you can call him Uncle Maddux. My mom and dad live an hour away. They will be coming up next weekend to see my new house. You can call them Grandma and Grandpa."

"I wanna see them," Harper says, apparently not falling asleep anytime soon. "When can we meet your brother, your mom, and your dad?"

Ryan's voice answers, "When you fall asleep, your mom and I will make a plan. We will tell you tomorrow." There is a silent pause. "Keep your eyes closed and roll over," he directs. "I will rub your backs like my mom used to rub mine at bedtime."

Five minutes pass before Christy joins me in the kitchen. I motion to a glass of wine poured for her beside mine on the counter.

"This was too big for you not to tell me, and you know it. You knew he would bump into me; you knew he would be here tonight, and you know…" Christy trails off as I raise an eyebrow.

"Want me to tell you about Friday? Or Saturday? Or Tuesday?"

She shakes her head. *She does, but she doesn't.*

"I need to know…" she begins right before Ryan joins us.

"Sorry to interrupt," he says.

"I will let the two of you chat," I say, smiling like the cat that ate the canary.

Leaning near Christy's ear, without touching her, I whisper, "Spoiler alert! Happy ending."

4

SUPER HERO TO ZERO

Brooks

I've dreaded Tuesday for a week now. Today will be rough for my bestie, but I've seen the happiness that awaits her from tomorrow on. I refresh my feed often, anxiously awaiting *The Back 9 Talk* blog post I predicted in my vision.

For this country club rumor blog's second post, they've hit gold with a scandal between a prestigious club member and the swimming pool manager. The blog's follower count skyrockets with talk of today's post. A sex scandal sells; this one has the bonus of the NFL's golden boy with five-year-old twins. It ignites controversy as many members love Christy and the girls at the pool in the summers. Ryan and Christy hooked up long before either came to the club, and they aren't actively having an affair while she's an employee. By the end of the day, an online petition seeks support to get Christy her job back.

Drama. Drama. Barack Obama.

I find it hard to be upset as I know the fairytale life in store for my friend. I do, however, detest the country club socialites and all their gossip.

I watch the computer mouse spin as it refreshes.

Ahh. There it is.

The Back 9 Talk

By now, we all know "Superman" and tight end for the KC Cardinals is our club's newest member and resident of Breakstone Cliffs. But did you know "Aqua Woman" hooked up with "Superman," and our very own "Wonder Twins" are actually his? It is a story over five years old, and I don't know about you, but I want ALL the details.

I already know rumors at the club will wreak havoc for my best friend today. I busy myself on two new sketches for clients as I wait for Christy to be fired, Ryan to find her cleaning out her desk, and the four of them to escape to Maddux's house behind the privacy gates. The clock on the wall seems to stand still. I'd go home, but there's nothing there to distract me.

I take my phone in hand, shooting off a text.

> ME
> I'm here if you need me
> I promise
> happily ever after

I turn my sketchpad to a new page, and I draw the twins at the park with Christy and Ryan. Christy and Ry sit on swings as Ryan and Harper push them. Wainwright, their future boxer, jumps and barks at their movement on the swings, causing laughter from the twins. Wide smiles adorn their faces as their curls fly in the breeze. I stare at my completed drawing until my cell phone vibrates on the counter beside me.

"What. The. Actual. Heck?" I ask in greeting, louder than I intended, pretending to be angry for her benefit.

"There is more," Christy tells me. "And you are on speakerphone."

"I saw *The Back 9 Talk* post," I state. "That did not help your case."

"She did nothing wrong." A male voice butts into our conversation.

"Well, hello. Is this Ryan?" I query.

"Yep," he replies.

"You should have given me a heads up about today," Christy grumbles.

"But you have a pesky rule about not wanting me to share," I remind her. "There are better things coming this week. Well, from today on, the future looks good for both of you," I promise.

"Let's wait until he gets to know you better before you scare him with your freaky gift." Christy chuckles hollowly.

"I am here to stay," Ryan declares.

I laugh through the phone. He has no idea how many years' worth of visions I've seen of him with Christy and the girls.

"I'm glad you are on the phone, Brooks. Maybe together, we can convince Christy to let me help her out financially," Ryan plots, enlisting my help as Christy's best friend.

I chuckle. "Go ahead and try. Act like I am not on the phone."

Ryan wastes no time. "I mean, legally, I owe Christy over five years of child support," I assume he looks to her. "Christy, please do not fight me. They are my daughters—my flesh and blood." He pauses for a moment.

"It kills me to think of you struggling to raise Harper and Ry on your own. You know me; you know the kind of man I am. They are my family. You are my family. I need to take care of the three of you. I need to help with finances, childcare, education, healthcare, and everything else. I missed too much. I do not plan to miss any more. I take my new role of being a father seriously, just like you do being their mom."

I imagine my friend is opening her mouth to argue, but Ryan stops her by continuing.

"I understand it is hard for you to allow me to help. You were a single parent, making every decision on your own." Ryan pauses. "I'm in the picture now and expect to make important decisions with you. I will not be a dick about it, but I will remind you, and I will contribute financially. You made your opinions known on Saturday. I listened and thought about it. I need you to hear me. I am the twins' father, and as their father, I have a responsibility."

My mind drifts. I long to drive to Maddux's home to be nearby and support Christy and the girls. *It's only been the four of us for nearly six years; it will be hard for me to allow Ryan to take my place. From today on, I am on the outside looking in. I am the friend, not the roommate. They become the family they always should have been while I...while I am sentenced to live alone, never to find the love they have.*

I exhale a long breath, reaching for the handle on the right of Ryan's large, oak double front door. I'm excited for Christy and the twins, but the extra cars in the driveway hint it won't be just the five of us this evening.

I emerge from the large foyer to find Maddux wrapping his arm around his brother's shoulders. "We will man the grill," he states, looking at Ryan for approval. "We men. We make fire. We grill." Maddux grunts like a neanderthal.

"I knew you were a barbarian," I barb, walking into the room.

Christy gives me a pointed stare, hoping I will refrain from causing a scene. I tend to speak my mind and stir things up. I'm sure she doesn't want this to happen around Ryan's family.

As Maddux and Ryan return to the deck and the grill area, Christy asks them to encourage the girls to climb out of the pool. She continues peeling apples and sipping beer while I watch. Soon, we hear the girls bound up the stairs.

"Mommy! Mommy!" they holler.

"Stop," she orders, and they freeze in place, towels wrapped around their shoulders. "Inside voices, please."

"Guess what," Harper says, approaching the counter opposite us.

I do not miss Ryan's parents pausing behind the twins, eyes locked on me. Coming here straight from work today, I didn't think perhaps I should change. My green, blue, and gold plaid, pleated mini skirt with thin black lines—paired with my skin-tight, black sweater vest, while normal for me, shocks them. I'm sure the spiked black collars at my neck and wrists, along with my black biker boots, are not commonly seen in their Overland Park Country Club and social circles. To most, I look scary with my tattoos and what some refer to as gothic attire; they'll probably judge me instantly.

"What?" Christy asks her girls, faking excitement.

"Gigi said we could spend the night at her house," Harper announces, a big smile upon her face.

This is not good. I know Christy, it's too soon.

"Breathe," I instruct, speaking low for only her to hear, my hands upon the countertop. "Make an excuse, take a minute, and step outside."

My friend nods. "I'm okay," she whispers.

"Wow! That is exciting." She pretends for her daughters' sake. "Do me a favor, girls. Go out and ask Daddy if the grill is ready for Mr. Josh."

Excited to tell their father their news, they jog onto the deck.

Barely a minute passes before a concerned Ryan makes his way back into the kitchen. Without a word, he strides toward Christy, places his hands at her hips, and lowers his mouth close to her ear.

"If it is too soon, say the word, and I will talk to my parents," he murmurs.

I feel I'm intruding on a private moment when Ryan catches me listening at Christy's side. I'm torn. I can't leave her; I fear she is not thrilled with the girls having a sleepover with his parents.

"I am okay," Christy whispers. "It...I...It caught me off guard. That's all."

"I will make an excuse that I want them to spend the first night in my house with my new furniture," Ryan offers.

"No," Christy says, a little louder than a whisper. "They are excited and want to spend time with your parents. I... I need to... I should let them go have fun."

"Then, we will have fun, too," I proclaim.

"Yeah," Ryan joins in, spinning Christy to face him. "Let's celebrate my new place. You, Brooks, and Maddux should stay over. We will party; we can break in the pool table. I have plenty of bedrooms when we all decide to crash."

Christy's tear-filled eyes pierce my heart. She hates the idea of Ryan's parents keeping the girls. *It is too soon. I see it written all over her face.*

"I need to let them go," she whispers shakily.

"I will keep you company," Ryan vows, and she nods.

"We will not leave you alone," I promise. "We will keep you busy until they come back tomorrow. We can make it a girls' night."

Christy nods, wiping her unshed tears from her eyes. She turns to face me.

"The apartment will only make me think of them," she confesses. "Will you stay here with me?"

I glance at Ryan, and he nods before I agree.

"I need to talk to your folks," Christy states. "And I need to pack their bags."

"Let's eat," I suggest. "Then you can talk while the girls pack their bags."

Ryan's approving smile warms me.

"Brother?" Maddux shouts from the deck through the open French doors. "Where are the burgers?"

"And the hotdogs?" Harper yells.

Christy laughs. "You'd better get to work, Dad."

She pushes him away, returning to the apples. I smile and shoo Ryan out. He quirks his head, assessing. I wink at him, letting him know I will take care of my best friend. He carries a tray full of meat and grilling utensils with him as he returns to the deck. Sending the twins to change from their swimsuits, I assume Ryan enlists Maddux's assistance in distracting Christy for the night. Maddux glances towards us through the open doors. Making eye contact with me, he quickly turns back to the grill.

5

MAN MEAT

Brooks

My eyes constantly on my best friend, I note Ryan catches Christy looking at the time on his cell phone. "They are already asleep." He says what she already knows. "I could call Mom and see how the night went."

As hope floods Christy's eyes, he connects a video call.

"Hello, dear," Jackie greets.

Christy waves from his side.

"Are the girls asleep?" he asks.

"Yes. See for yourself." Though I cannot see the video phone screen, I assume she turns the camera toward the sleeping twins. "The girls were angels. You must let them stay over again soon."

"Of course. They will want to visit you often," Christy lies. All she wants is to keep them all to herself for months to come. She's never away from them overnight.

They discuss drop off in the morning then disconnect the call.

"They are fine; they are asleep." Ryan keeps his voice low. "Let's have fun while they sleep, and tomorrow morning, we will find the twins here bright and early," he promises.

Christy only nods. I make it my mission to distract her tonight. It's my job as best friend to see that she enjoys the night off from being a mom. Christy has only been away from the girls while they were at school and she was at work or had fallen sick with the flu. This is her first mom's night out.

She deserves a fun night with adults.

"Drink up," I prompt, slipping a shot glass into each of our hands. "The girls are safe. We are awake and not at work, so let's drink," I urge, on the brink of a demand.

"Is that what you consider a toast?" Maddux asks, chuckling.

"Can you do better?" I challenge.

"Whoa," Ryan orders. "One toast per shot."

He holds his little shot glass higher. We follow his lead then down the shot. Christy's body sputters as she gasps for breath, her tongue and throat on fire. Ryan and Maddux chortle loudly at her discomfort. She rolls her eyes at them.

"What shall we play first?" I ask, scanning the game room.

"Darts," Ryan says at the same time Maddux says, "Air hockey."

Christy and I exchange a look and giggle. We don't want to play either option.

"I would prefer we play darts before you drink much more," Ryan tells his brother.

"That only happened one time," Maddux laughs. "And it was at my house."

I turn towards Christy, rolling my eyes. She laughs. Not sure how to really play darts, we attempt to mess the guys up on each throw. While all Christy can do is laugh, I easily get under Maddux's skin, and his game suffers, or so Ryan says.

Upon his defeat, Maddux pours four shots.

"Ryan, break the rules. C'mon," he encourages, shot glass extended.

"What does he mean by 'break the rules'?" Christy asks, nudging his shoulder.

Ryan's blue eyes melt into hers. "I only have two drinks," he shares.

"Why?" I ask.

"A long time ago, I had too many, and I hurt someone I cared about. So, I only allow myself two drinks."

He holds up two fingers between Christy and him. Her breath hitches.

"Really?" she croaks.

"Yes," Maddux answers, disgusted. "Since you are here tonight, can you forgive him so he will enjoy another drink with us?"

My hand flies to my heart. Tears well in Christy's eyes at his gesture.

"C'mon, man." Maddux wiggles the shot glass as he begs.

"Only for tonight. I will have more than two drinks, because you are here and no one plans to leave," Ryan's eyes lock on my friend's. "If you are okay with it."

She nods.

"Hey, hey," he coos.

"Whoa! I did not mean to kill the party mood," Maddux modulates louder than necessary.

"Shots," I say, hoping for a distraction. "Shots will help."

Christy looks wearily at me.

"No twins, no work, and no driving. We are drinking," I cheer.

All four of us throw back our shots of whiskey.

"High five," Maddux prompts, palm in the air, extended toward me. "A much better toast."

I hesitate for a moment, remember he blocks my visions, then give him a high five.

I smile wide at Christy. I have finally found someone I may touch and not worry about seeing visions. It seems foreign, allowing myself to make contact in a simple high five. With Ryan in the girls' and Christy's lives, Maddux and I will be seeing each other often. *We should become friends or act like we get along.*

"We should play pool, girls against boys," I announce, causing Christy to quirk a brow.

"Uh," Ryan hedges.

"We have a table in the back room of the tattoo parlor. We can hold our own," I assure, patting my palm against Maddux's chest.

I touched him again. I'm not sure why I touched him; it's weird. I fight a laugh. *I'm weird for not touching others, and I'm weird when I do touch someone.*

"Game on," Maddux states, clapping his hands loudly one time.

I hand Christy a fresh beer as we approach the pool table. I lean near her side and whisper, "Take it easy the first game. We will run the table for the second one."

She nods. Ryan breaks; no balls fall into a pocket. I play with the pool cue in my hand, getting comfy with the feel of it. I address the white ball, line up my shot, and sink the nine-ball in the center pocket.

"Yay! We are stripes," I cheer, shifting my hips from side to side playfully.

Christy bites her lips to keep from laughing hysterically at me. I do not act like this. Ever. My friend knows I am playing this up for the guys because I'm nowhere near my drink limit.

I sink one more ball before scratching. Maddux expertly removes three solid balls from the table before missing his fourth shot. Christy glances at me and then Ryan, who smiles supportively. She sinks two balls before purposefully flubbing up her third shot.

"Losers do shots," Maddux states confidently before Ryan's turn.

"Nooo," Christy answers, shaking her head. "This is just a practice game."

The guys stare at her, trying to ascertain if she is serious.

"Practice is over," I announce. "Maddux, rack 'em up. Let's start the real game."

Ryan fetches four beers while Maddux racks the balls on the pool table.

"Let's make it interesting," I say, winking in my friend's direction. "But first, let's fix this."

I approach Maddux, extending my arms and messing up his perfectly styled hair. His eyes bug out, and shock sweeps across his face. When he lifts his hands to attempt to restyle his hair, I swat them away.

"Trust me. It looks better," I declare. "But you are so uptight, I bet you can't leave it like this for the rest of the night."

Tight lips and squinted eyes display his anger.

Unbothered by his reaction, I turn to a smiling Ryan and Christy.

"How about we play strip pool?" I suggest, causing Christy to nearly sputter beer onto the black felt cover of the table.

Ryan's head snaps in her direction. I am not sure if his eyes flash with fear or hope.

"What are the rules?" Maddux inquires, as if it has been decided.

Ryan leans into Christy, murmuring, "I'm game if you are."

I am not sure if it is the alcohol in her system or the glimmer in Ryan's eye that spurs her on.

"We remove one article of clothing at the end of our turn," she suggests.

Ryan's blue eyes liquify, and his pupils dilate. "Really?" he asks.

"Really," she states, surveying the group and mentally counting clothes.

Both guys wear t-shirts and shorts. So, with her bra, Christy wears one more piece of clothing than they do.

"Guys break," Christy instructs, faking her bravado.

Not wanting us to back out, Maddux points his pool cue, breaks, and balls scatter in all directions. Two solid balls and one stripe now rest in pockets.

"We will take solids," Maddux announces, lining up his next shot.

His cue nearly misses the white ball entirely, causing us to laugh as he removes his shirt, folds it neatly, and places it on a nearby barstool. I look at Christy, and I feel my eyes bug out. I thought it was a fantasy while sketching; I did not expect him to really be so muscular with a trim waist.

"You're up," Maddux challenges me.

I shake my head. "Christy will go next," I suggest, looking at my friend.

I watch as Christy wastes no time lining up a shot. When the white ball clanks against a striped ball, dropping it into the pocket, we cheer. She perfectly placed the white ball in line for her next shot. Christy taps two more balls in before missing.

Ryan licks his lips in anticipation. *I fear I delivered my friend's bare body to him on a silver platter.*

Christy's fingers grasp the hem of her shirt, hesitating instead of lifting it over her head. Her fingers move to the button then the zipper of her shorts before sliding them slowly down her thighs.

I laugh to myself. *There is no way the men will be able to make a shot with our bare skin nearby.*

"Earth to Ryan," Maddux calls, interrupting his fantasies. "You are up."

He moves around the pool table, appraising each angle, looking for the shot he knows he can make. He finds it hard to think; his eyes keep darting to Christy's thighs. *This will be easier than I anticipated.*

Ryan stands to the left of Christy, lines up, and taps a ball into the corner pocket. Of course, he misses his next attempt and removes his shirt.

"Yummy, yummy." I lick my lips playfully. "How will I ever concentrate with so much man meat on display?"

Christy rolls her eyes at me. I add a little extra sway to my hips as I move to the other side of the table and take my shot. Our purple-striped ball falls into the center pocket on my first shot, and I miss my second.

I promptly lift my black shirt over my head, tossing it onto the pile of discarded clothes. Comfortable in my body, I place my hands upon my hips, not hiding my exposed, tattooed skin or my lacy black bra.

Maddux chews on his lower lip, his eyes stuck on my breasts—which nearly pop out of my bra—and the intricate designs of my many tattoos. Ryan smirks, watching his brother's reaction.

"Bro," Ryan calls. "Earth to Maddux."

"Huh?" His brother shakes away the lust-filled haze, suddenly aware we are watching him.

He closes his eyes as he draws in a long breath through his nose. When he opens his eyes, it is easy to see he is fighting the urge to ogle me some more. He knocks in two solid balls before missing horribly on his third shot. The four of us laugh for several minutes at his huge mistake.

Ryan clenches his jaw, studying the table. He attempts to focus on the balls remaining and not on Christy, who is bending at the waist, her butt sticking out. He struggles more when she pumps her cue through her fingers before knocking the white ball into a striped ball on the table. Moving in slow motion, it rolls to the edge of the pocket, seems to hover for a moment, then tumbles out of sight.

This leaves only one striped ball and the eight-ball on the table. *Two expert shots from Christy and we win.* She lines up her shot, closes her eyes for a moment as if in prayer, then takes it. Although perfectly planned, she neglects to hit it hard enough. The striped ball stops rolling an inch from the center pocket.

Christy points her index finger across the table at me. "This is all your fault," she reminds me before turning her back to us and removing her t-shirt.

After tossing it on the pile, she turns back toward the pool table. Unlike me, she's uncomfortable with so much on display. Her hands on opposite shoulders, her elbows and forearms cover most of her chest.

When she attempts to move to the end of the table, Ryan snakes his arm around her abdomen, pulling her back towards him. Even though he caught her off guard, she does not fight him.

"So. Damn. Hot," he growls into her ear.

She tenses. Not wanting to upset her, he releases his hold. She spins. Nearly nose to nose with him, she smirks.

"So, you like what you see?" she teases. "This is all you get. Brooks will finish the game, we will win, and all of this..." she motions her hand up and down her body, "...will disappear."

She turns around, snags her beer, and takes a sip, no longer attempting to cover herself. She moves in the way of Ryan's next shot. He grips her waist, guiding her from his left side to his right. Trying to remain in control, he quickly releases her, taking his pool cue in hand.

"Concentrate," Maddux urges from across the table, pulling Ryan back to the game.

"Do not miss," Christy murmurs huskily while leaning into his side.

Before him is an easy shot, but he messes it up.

He turns toward Christy as he unbuttons his shorts and lowers his zipper. Her mouth forms an "O" as she watches him slide his shorts down his thighs then step out of them.

6

50-50 CHANCE

Brooks

Ryan stands between Christy and the pool table in only his snug, gray boxer briefs. She stares as he cups and adjusts himself. There is no place to hide in briefs. A squeal escapes when, in the blink of an eye, he grabs Christy's wrist and pulls her flush against him.

"Like what you see?" he whispers, his lips brushing her ear.

Christy lifts her right palm to his chest and presses firmly against his hard muscles, urging him to turn back to the game. Caught up in their own interactions, they miss Maddux's turn and find him standing proudly in his boxers, emptying his beer.

"My turn," I announce, cue already in hand.

I wink at my friend, sinking the last striped ball. Like I'd planned, the white ball sets me up for the next shot.

"Eight-ball in the center pocket," I call, pointing to the other side of the table.

The balls smack together, and the black eight-ball drops into the correct pocket. I take two steps towards Christy, clapping and cheering.

When we finish cheering, I lean in, whispering, "I am commando."

I watch her expression change as she realizes that means I stand before her in only my bra and skirt. Had I missed on my last shot, I would stand only in my plaid skirt.

"I knew we would win." I tap my temple, letting her know I saw the outcome in a vision.

"Beat ya," I taunt the men.

"Time for more shots," Maddux announces, eyes glued on me.

"Clothes first. Shots second," Christy commands.

Standing at the pile of clothes, Ryan passes my shirt to me, then Christy her shirt and shorts.

"Time to do two more shots," I whisper into Christy's ear. This causes her to pull her eyes from Ryan and adamantly shake her head no.

"Two shots are better than one," Maddux declares, proudly displaying eight shot glasses atop the bar.

"Told you!" I yell. "Why do you ever doubt me?"

"I don't doubt you," Christy grumbles under her breath. "I don't want to take two more shots."

"My house, my rules," Maddux proclaims.

"Um, it's my house," Ryan clarifies.

Maddux thinks about it for a minute then chuckles.

"Line up, ladies and gents," Maddux invites, sliding one shot glass closer to each of us.

"Whose turn to toast?" Ryan asks, scanning the group.

Christy and I hold empty shot glasses inches from our lips, having already downed one each.

"You didn't see that one coming?" Christy asks me.

"What's with all the talking in code about predictions?" Ryan asks, looking at us beside him.

We share a conspiratorial look.

"Bottoms up," I goad, my second shot glass in hand.

Maddux and Ryan shoot two shots in record time, slamming the empty glasses on the bar between them. They do not let my changing the subject distract them.

"Glasses are empty, so now you must answer," Ryan urges. "The predictions."

"I need to sit down," Christy groans, trudging toward the large leather sofa.

Ryan tilts his head in her direction, and we follow him to join her. He plops down on the opposite end, leaning against the arm of the sofa. Maddux claims the recliner, and I force myself into the tiny space to the left of Christy, causing her to move within a foot of Ryan.

"Should I tell them?" I whisper, loud enough everyone can hear.

"Tell us what?" Maddux inquires.

All eyes move to me.

"Brooks has a gift," Christy announces, eyes ping-ponging between Maddux and Ryan.

"You brought us a gift?" Maddux asks, slurring a bit.

"No, stupid," Ryan corrects, frustrated, also slurring his words.

"I have the gift of sight," I declare.

"I hate to burst your bubble, but all four of us can see," Maddux deadpans.

"Will you shut up?" Ryan growls.

"She's not making sense," Maddux complains in return.

"She has visions that predict the future," Christy states with a huff.

Maddux must be annoying her, too.

"When I touch someone, I experience flashes," I share. "I see events for that person."

"So, when we high five, you can see my future?" Maddux asks, disbelieving.

"If I hug Christy or high five Ryan, I will see a vision," I explain. "I can't control it."

"How does that work during tattoos?" Ryan asks.

"At work, I keep my gloves on at all times." I reposition myself, tucking my legs beside me on the sofa cushion. "Though I try, I can't avoid all contact and visions."

"How so?" Ryan slurs.

"It is impossible to keep the twins from hugging or holding her hand," Christy states. "Sometimes, strangers bump into her in public. That kind of thing."

"What's in the visions?" Maddux inquires.

"I see dates, parties, holidays, illnesses, visitors, vacations…"

"Death?" Maddux interrupts.

I nod. "I can't choose to only see happy visions. What plays in my mind is random."

"So, you know everything that will happen to Christy and you," Maddux continues, very interested in this topic of conversation.

I shake my head at the same time Christy answers, "I asked that she not share visions she has for the girls and me."

"Occasionally, I am in a vision with the person I am touching, but I can't see my own future. I only see their past and future, and I might be present when it happens." My shoulders rise and fall with a deep breath.

"You have no control over it?" Ryan asks.

"Nope," I respond. "Well, maybe I do. Something weird happened last week."

When no one speaks, I continue. "The other day, two guys came in. I had my gloves on, standing behind the counter. While I sketched a design, one of the men reached to point at the paper. His fingers grazed my forearm for just a second."

I share a look with Christy.

"That's the only time a stranger touched me, and I did not experience a vision," I confess.

"And you did not know the guy?" Maddux asks.

"It was you, dummy," Christy laughs.

"Prove it," Maddux challenges, extending his hand.

"I touched you twice at the shop and gave you high fives tonight, and I get no visions from you," I tell him.

"So, touch Ryan or touch Christy," he urges.

"I don't need to," I announce. "I shook Ryan's hand at the tattoo parlor. I saw plenty."

"So, tell me something that has not happened yet so I can believe you when it happens," Maddux commands.

"Come with me," I order, waving my hand for Maddux to hurry up.

We disappear down the hall for less than a minute, then return.

"Let's watch a movie," Maddux suggests.

"Beer run," Ryan announces. "Who wants one?"

Christy raises her hand while Maddux and I say, "Me."

"Hey. You okay?" Christy asks, approaching Ryan, who is behind the bar.

I listen closely, not needing to watch my vision unfold. Unlike me, Maddox watches every movement from the sofa. His hand clutches my forearm, and he squeezes as the vision comes to fruition.

"Told you!" I announce.

"I'm a believer," Maddox states, not pulling his eyes from Christy and his brother as he rises and walks toward them.

"Dude," Maddux excitedly calls at the bar, only a couple feet away. "She said you would kiss Christy."

"There was a 50 percent chance we would kiss tonight," Ryan scoffs.

Christy swats his chest.

"Well, probably more like an 80 or 90 percent chance," he teases.

Maddux shakes his head. "Brooks said the two of you would kiss behind the bar tonight before we turned on the movie. She even knew we would be watching *Die Hard*. Dude, that is my favorite movie!"

Ryan squints his eyes at me.

"I am so jealous," Maddux announces, causing all of us to furrow our brows at him.

"Jealous that she does not have visions of me," he clarifies. "Unlike Christy, I would want to know all about them."

7

PLEASE DON'T LET THERE BE A THIRD

Brooks

Maddux grabs my wrist, halting me outside the guest room. "Sooo..."

"Sooo?" I return, leaning myself against the door frame to the room I chose.

Standing before me, Maddux's large frame wobbles from side to side. I can't be sure if it's my alcohol-induced blurry vision or if it's his alcohol consumption causing him to stumble. I press my palms to the wooden frame to refrain from reaching out to steady him.

"We could..." he implies, his eyes moving toward the bedroom behind me.

"We could what?" I huff, exasperated by him talking in code.

He extends his hand, placing his palm next to my face on the wall.

"We should keep the party going in your room or mine," he suggests.

"You think so, do you?" I chuckle.

"I know so," he counters, pressing his free hand to my abdomen, encouraging me into the guest room behind me.

My eyes roam his body. *This big guy is packing.* My fuzzy brain reels as I stumble backwards until my calves connect with the bed. I experience no visions with Maddux. I could have fun with him in our inebriated state and brush it off as a one-night stand. *I've waited so long for intimacy without the distraction of my visions—too long. Now I'm a 23-year-old virgin, clumsy and suddenly unsure of myself.*

I reach to the nightstand and my open overnight bag.

"Here," I say and thrust a bottle of lotion into his chest. "You and your manaconda go party in your own room."

Maddux's hand covers mine and the bottle as he laughs at my comment. "Manaconda, huh?"

"It's definitely not a garter snake," I explain. "Now, go." I point to the door, my hands shoving him away.

He looks past my hands toward his groin then up to my face before he places my lotion back in my bag and exits my room, shutting the door behind him.

I fall to the mattress behind me, allowing a large breath to escape. My blurry eyes struggle to focus on the faint lights dancing upon the ceiling from the tiny window. I struggle to open my eyes each time I blink. I fight the urge to keep them shut. I raise my hands to my face, trailing my fingertips lightly over my cheeks down my chin and neck. *The sensation feels...divine.* I skim my fingers down my collarbone.

I need...

"Maaddduuxx," I whisper into the darkness.

Maddux

Manaconda...Brooks words play over and over in my mind. At the same time, I berate myself for pressing her for more tonight. I love that she acknowledged she checked me out. The more she pushes back and the more she antagonizes me, the more attractive I find her.

I am not sure what it is exactly about her that does it for me, but she pushes all my buttons in a big way. Her green eyes tend to wrap around me, pulling me towards her. I long to fist my fingers in her coal black hair and trace over her many tattoos. *She is the polar opposite of the women I hook up with... Maybe that is it. She is not at all the type I fall into bed with.*

Brooks

"What the hell?" Christy nudges me awake on her way to her duffle bag.

"I did not wake you up," I gripe defensively.

"No, but you did leave me sleeping on the couch with Ryan all night," Christy growls, toothbrush in hand.

Walking behind her, she tracks my movements in the mirror. I shrug before lowering the sleep shorts I borrowed from her to pee.

"His mom and the girls will be here in 20 minutes," Christy informs. "There is no way she will not think I got drunk and slept with her baby boy again last night."

"First, he's no baby boy," I say, flushing the stool. "Second, he is an adult, and who he chooses to sleep with is none of her G-D business." With my hip, I push Christy from the sink to wash my hands. "And third..."

"Please do not let there be a third. I am too hungover for it," my friend whines.

"And third," I drawl out, "I will make you bright-eyed and bushy-tailed before she arrives."

"There is not enough fairy dust to rid me of this headache," she warns.

"Swallow," I instruct, hand extended with two pain relievers in my palm.

Christy takes the proffered pills and the bottle of water from my other hand to wash them down with.

"Shower," I order, index finger pointed.

"Breakfast is served," I call from the vanity five minutes later.

Stepping from the shower stall, Christy inspects the two pieces of toast and a small glass of juice waiting on her. She awards me a smile, grateful I have her back this morning. She allows me to apply a quick swipe of eye liner and a coat of mascara on her eyes. Then she secures her long hair in a high ponytail.

"Maddux is cleaning the game room and bar. I think Ryan is showering upstairs," I inform casually, large smile climbing onto my face. I waggle my eyebrows at her.

"Stop it," she chides. "There was alcohol involved."

"Happy ending," I state, hinting not for the first time to the visions I experienced after shaking Ryan's hand.

"Cut that out," Christy warns, pointing her finger at me. "I do not share your gift, but I'd be blind not to see what is developing between Maddux and you."

My face burns like fire, and my lip snarls.

"Ready?" I snip.

Christy nods, following me from our guest room. She waves at Maddux, who is loading a dishwasher behind the bar, unable to fight her grin. We barely clear the top step when the front door bursts wide open, and the girls run inside. Christy opens her arms, but they run into the kitchen to the waiting arms of their father.

They talk a mile a minute, sharing everything they did at their grandparents' house while he crouches, and they hug his neck. Standing in the open doorway, his mother clutches her hand to her heart, tears filling her eyes.

"Christy?" Ryan's mother calls.

"Hmm?" she mumbles.

"They were angels, but now we realize why we parent children when we are young," Jackie chuckles. "We are exhausted."

Christy smiles. "So, you had a good night?"

"Of course," she croons. "You raised perfect little angels. They even helped with the dishes."

Next to me, Christy finds herself wrapped in Jackie's arms as she murmurs so low, I can barely hear, "Thank you for keeping them safe and healthy. Thank you for loving Ryan enough to give them his name. You allowed him to play the game he loves while you gave up so much, and we can never thank you enough."

When Christy is released, tears in her eyes, her girls smile up at her, and Ryan looks on with wide, worried eyes. She forces a small smile upon her mouth.

I feel I need to lighten the mood.

"Who wants their picture to be the first to hang on Ryan's fridge?" I ask the room.

"Me!" Ry yells.

"I do!" Harper argues.

"Well, where should we draw?" I inquire of the girls.

"There!" they yell and point to the new table in Ryan's eat-in kitchen.

Josh and Christy quickly supply paper, crayons, and markers. The twins talk excitedly about the pictures they plan to draw, and the adults discuss lunch plans.

I feel as if I'm intruding in this newly formed family, so I make an excuse and exit, but I don't go home. I busy myself with miscellaneous work tasks, not eager to return to my apartment, knowing I will be living alone from now on.

8
BIASED MUCH

Brooks

"Got a second?" Christy asks, walking into the back room of my tattoo parlor.

Looking up at her from my office chair, I bite my lips, a smile peeking through. *Here it comes.*

"What's up, buttercup?" I ask, popping the "P."

"I know it is fast..."

My best friend struggles to speak. I interrupt her. "We knew the day would come when you would leave my nest." I shrug, making light of this big, life-changing event.

"You knew," she accuses. "This was one of the visions."

I nod, a wide smile upon my face.

"So, do you know where he and the girls are right now?" she questions.

"Nope."

"Maddux and Ryan took the twins and their new golf clubs to the driving range at the club," Christy informs me. "I am picking up a few toys and clothes. Then I am supposed to join them."

This news lifts me from my seat. I pace to the window, hands on my hips.

"Are you going to the club?" I ask.

"Ryan's keen on us using his family membership," she explains.

"How do you feel about returning there after they…"

"Fired me?" she finishes. "I'm over it."

Christy stands beside me, looking out the window to the alley behind the parlor.

"That being said, it will be awkward," she admits. "I expect members to whisper about me when they see us."

"So, you plan to be a member?" I ask.

"Let's take it one step at a time," she chuckles. "Today, I will watch the girls at the driving range. Want to come over tomorrow and help me set up the twins' bedroom?"

Maddux

It is a beautiful, sunny summer day with a slight breeze. The clanking of clubs on the opposite side of Ryan demands my attention.

"Surprise." Christy fakes her enthusiasm. "Paige dropped me off."

Ryan looks around the range and parked carts for Paige.

Not spotting her, he turns to face Christy. "You found the clothes." He motions toward her attire.

"Funny thing. They were in *your* closet." She laces her voice with sarcasm.

He smiles sheepishly. "I knew you would want to play with the girls, so I made sure you were ready."

Moving to stand in the space behind the twins, Christy asks, "How are they doing?"

"They are naturals," I announce, smiling.

"Mommy!" the girls squeal, running to her with clubs in hand.

"Shhh!" Christy admonishes.

"Remember what we talked about," Ryan directs. "We use inside voices on the golf course."

The girls nod.

"We do not want to mess up the other golfers," Ry explains to me.

"That is right," Christy agrees. "Show me what Uncle Maddux and Daddy taught you. Ry, you show me first," she instructs.

We watch as both girls place their balls on a wooden tee. Ry turns her golf ball, so the logo faces her; Harper doesn't worry about hers. Ry places her three-wood behind the ball and spreads her feet apart. Her little chest rises and falls as she steadies her breath before swinging. She connects solidly. With a loud *ting*, her ball takes flight, landing about 100 yards away. She smiles proudly, and we award her with a golf clap.

"My turn," Harper announces, her driver already positioned behind her ball.

She holds her breath as she draws her long club back then swings it forward, striking the ball, sending the tee flying with it. Her drive lands past the red 100-yard flag in front of us. Harper hugs her dad before looking at Christy for her approval.

"Wow! I think you hit better than Mommy," Christy tells the girls, only half teasing.

"You'd better practice, Mommy," Harper states.

"I will practice if the two of you keep practicing," she encourages. "Hit some," she prompts the girls. "I will watch while I stretch."

Christy grabs her nine-iron, placing her hands on each end. Raising it above her head, she stretches her arms and back. She watches closely as the twins move to their irons, listen to Ryan and me, then swing two times. They are little pros, and it's only their first time with clubs in their hands.

Christy adjusts her grip and stance multiple times, no doubt feeling our gaze upon her. Bending her legs slightly, she swings. I'm surprised; the ball arches high and lands in the circle around the red flag.

"Not bad," I state from behind her.

"Bro, did you say, 'Not bad'?" Ryan chides. "That was great! Nine-iron, right?"

Christy nods.

"One hundred yards with a nine-iron for the first time in six years is spectacular!" Ryan cheers.

"Biased much?" I tease.

Christy points her club in my direction. I raise my arms, returning to the girls. As I assist them, I occasionally watch Christy hit with each of her irons. *She's got a great swing.*

"Two more hits each," I coach the twins.

They quickly swing two more times. Harper throws the strap of her bag over her shoulder, and Ry allows me to carry her clubs to the cart for her. Christy secures her bag in the empty slot on the back of my cart, allowing the girls to return home with Ryan.

"I am proud of you," I state, pressing the gas pedal.

"Me? Why?" she asks.

"It was not easy for you to join us today, but you did it." I do not look her way as I follow Ryan's cart up the path. "It means a lot to Ryan to do these things with the girls, and he told me he's worried about you."

I feel her stare on my profile.

"He wants you to enjoy all that the club has to offer and not let the loophole they quoted in letting you go deter you," I share with a glance in her direction. "So, I am proud of you for joining us on the driving range today. By the looks of it, the twins get their golfing skills from you."

"Ryan golfs," she argues.

"Not very well," I chuckle.

"He's out of practice. That's all," she argues.

I smirk, at her defense of my brother.

"What did Ryan tell you today?" she asks.

"About what?" I inquire.

"About the girls and me," she answers. "Did he tell you we are moving in with him?"

"Do you want to move in with Ryan?" I refuse to answer her question.

"The twins living with Ryan is how it should be," she states.

"That is not what I asked."

"It is fast," she admits.

"For who? For the girls? For you?" I counter.

"Don't *you* think it is fast?"

"Christy, it does not matter what I think. It does not matter what my parents think. It does not matter what members at the club think. All that matters is the twins, Ryan, and you," I say, parking my cart in Ryan's driveway.

She nods.

I lower my voice. "Do you want to move in with Ryan?" A tender smile forms on my face.

"I do," she murmurs.

I wrap my arm behind her shoulders, squeezing her. "Good. Because Ryan loves you. And…" I drawl low, for only us to hear. "…I knew you were moving in with Ryan on Friday night."

She begins to ask how when I explain, "Brooks told me when you "camped out" Thursday night with Ryan that you officially moved in with him and would not be returning to her apartment. She said you just didn't know it yet." I chuckle. "She really does see the future."

9

FAMILY ONLY

Brooks

Hours pass slowly. Late in the afternoon, my cell signals a text.

CHRISTY
join us for dinner tonight
please
Josh grilling us pizza
Please say yes

ME
yes
be there soon

While I'm all for spending time with Ryan, Christy, and the girls, I hope Maddux won't be joining us.

Brooks

Maddux

"Thank you for inviting me for dinner," Brooks greets Ryan and Christy as she walks onto the deck overlooking the backyard.

"Yo, I thought this was for family only," I protest.

Brooks opens her mouth to put me in my place, but Ryan speaks first.

"Brooks is Christy's adopted sister," he states.

"I thought they were just friends." I tilt my head, looking in Christy's direction.

"They are closer than best friends," Ryan informs. "Brooks is family." His tone leaves no room for argument.

Brooks's eyes narrow, and her lip snarls in my direction. The saying "if looks could kill" comes to mind. She's shooting daggers at me. When I break my eyes from her, turning my attention to my brother, I feel the heat of her gaze on the side of my face.

Immediately upon taking our seats, Ryan raises his glass. "My favorite people surround this table. In planning this house, I envisioned moments like this. Now, this is my reality, and I look forward to making it a permanent occurrence." He gestures to toast, and he takes a drink.

I make a mental note to attempt to keep my comments about Brooks to a minimum. Clearly, she's a permanent fixture in Christy's life, and it seems the second part of her prediction last night will come to fruition. *Ryan's love for Christy radiates from every part of him. I thought him crazy to pine for her the past six years, but witnessing the love they share, I now understand. What they have is special; it's what my parents have. It's a once in a lifetime connection that I doubt I'll ever experience. Lightning struck twice in my family; there's no way it will strike a third time for me.*

Hot off the grill, Josh's homemade cheese, pepperoni, and supreme pizzas grace the center of the table. Ryan, Christy, the twins, Brooks, and Josh join me in fixing our plates.

As we eat, conversation flows. I note the twins lean their heads on their arms, and their eyes grow heavy. They've had a big two days, meeting the family, sleeping over at my parents, and swimming today.

Movement at my left catches my attention. I watch Brooks lean near Christy, whispering in her ear, and Christy's eyes grow wide as she shakes her head at her friend. Looking in first Ryan's then my direction, her eyes dart away when they find us watching her. I glance at Brooks, and she winks at me.

What is she up to now?

10

DID YOU SMELL ME?

Brooks

"Are you sure you want to do this?" I fold my fishnet-clad legs toward my chest and lean back on the pillows adorning Christy's bed. *I'm going to hate it when she's gone.* It's Sunday. Ryan's been in her life for only one week now.

Christy heaves a half-full moving box beside me on the comforter and wipes the sweat from her brow. She gives me a wink and flashes a smile that's usually comforting, but today, it's only making me nauseous. My best friend and her family are moving out. My apartment will be empty without the three of them.

I'm not ready for this.

I say that like I'm not already 23 with a trust fund and my own tattoo studio. By all accounts, I've got the perfect life.

Almost. Except for my ability to see. There's that.

And my inability to have meaningful physical contact with anyone... ever...because of it. There's that.

"We've gone over this already. I'm—"

"In love with Ryan. I know," I grumble, trying to keep the disappointment from my voice. A sigh escapes my pouty bottom lip, ruffling the black bangs which swoop across my forehead. *It's time to dye it again.* My roots are starting to show through the black.

"She'd better be anyway." Ryan steps into the bedroom, hoisting a box of his own, Christy's twin girls right behind him like little shadows. He kisses Christy on the cheek, and she turns toward him before turning back to her closet.

"Yeah, yeah, yeah." I roll my eyes.

Don't get me wrong; I'm happy for them. Even though Christy just stumbled into Ryan after over six years of being apart, she's never seemed happier. The twins are ecstatic about having "Daddy" around, and Ryan seems like one of the good ones.

Of course, I saw it coming. Despite knowing me for as long as she did, Christy didn't believe me. I guess she thought happiness wasn't going to be in the cards for her and the girls. Thankfully, she was wrong.

"What are these things?" asks a deeper voice from the hallway.

Ugh. Not him.

I cringe, expecting him to walk into the room dangling one of my black lace thongs in front of his face. *Did I do laundry this week? Wait, no. He has no reason to have been in my room.*

Maddux is…something. Yes, he's handsome. No. That's not it. Immaculate—that's a better word. From his blond curly hair to the sharp cut of his jaw, how every piece of clothing he owns seems to be tailored especially for him… He excites me, but at the same time, I can't stand him. He's *too* perfect.

Maddux lives in the Lynks at the Tryst Falls Country Club, a gated community with well-manicured lawns and stunning homes. Ryan built a home just down the road from his, a home to which he's whisking away Christy and the twins today.

This little apartment over my tattoo studio simply won't be the same without all the noise a single mom and her two kids can make. *I suppose I'll be lonely.*

With tears stinging the backs of my eyes, I turn toward Maddux, praying my eyeliner and mascara don't run.

My tarot cards. Why does he have those? Now, I'll need to do a cleansing ritual.

"Umm, those are mine." I stand up quickly, almost tripping over my black leather boots on the floor beside Christy's former bed.

"I didn't ask *whose* they were. I asked *what* they were," Maddux says as a rebuttal, holding the deck of cards slightly out of my reach.

There's a mischievous glint in his eyes that I can't quite read. It's almost a challenge. His jaw tenses, muscles flexing in his stubbled cheek and along the taut thickness of his neck. I reach toward my tarot cards, the three-quarter sleeve of my T-shirt riding a little bit above my elbow with the stretch, and he traces the tattoos on my forearm with his eyes.

Those long lashes. *I'm jealous.* Standing this close to him, I'm overwhelmed by the masculinity of his scent—a woodsy, musky cologne. *It's delicious. He's delicious.*

And okay, maybe it's making me a little hot.

Does he know?

Can he tell?

No. He's just a butthead. I know his type.

Never mind. It doesn't matter.

"Did you just smell me?" He now wears a knowing smirk.

My eyes narrow, and fire ignites in my belly. I turn my gaze upwards. I stand on my tiptoes and quickly snatch my tarot cards out of his hand. But just as he releases them, I lose my balance and stumble against his chest. My free hand lands against his firm pec, and he grabs my elbow to help steady me.

I gasp.

11

THAT'S WHAT I DO

Maddux

    Her green eyes bore into mine, and a flush of anger melts into the subtle blush of her cheeks. *I'd like to say the heavy eyeliner detracts from it all—it's certainly not what I usually go for—but oh man, it doesn't. Brooks is hot, a total rebel, and I think a part of me has wanted her since the first day Ryan and I walked into her tattoo shop.*
    I didn't expect her to gasp and jerk away so quickly when she fell against me. *Let's just say it's not the reaction I usually get. I meet a lot of women. Not one of them has been as confusing as Brooks.*
    She clears her throat and crosses her arms over her chest. *The tattoos are nice. Full sleeves—some pieces colorful and others shades of black.* I know she didn't do them herself, but she's talented in her own right. *I've seen her work. I can't wait for her to start on my tattoo. What am I thinking? Tattooed women aren't my thing, and neither are short little plaid skirts like the one barely covering her body right now.*
    Yeah. Brooks is trouble.
    Ryan's giving me a look like he knows what I'm thinking. He raises an eyebrow when I make eye contact, but I just shake my head and fight the urge to roll my eyes. *I don't want him to get any wild ideas.*

I have one-night stands.

That's what I do.

That's all I do.

I don't want a relationship. Not right now. Not when business has me so preoccupied. Not when there's so much at stake.

Yes, it might be fun to take the little minx around for a spin or two, but I'm not like Ryan. I don't want to settle down and play house with twins and a wifey. I'm built differently. My nights are occupied with business, poker games, and the women I meet off the dating apps. Of course, I don't really date them. It's just physical. That's all I'm offering. One-night stands to keep me focused on the work I do.

That's all.

Brooks, though, she seems different. She's Christy's best friend, and Ryan's my little brother. They'd kill me if they thought I used her like that.

But really, she'd be using me, too, right?

And I'd definitely make it worth her while.

"I'm exhausted. I hate moving. Promise we never have to do this again," Christy whines.

Ryan chuckles. "Good thing I literally just built you and the girls a massive house. We don't have to move again unless you want us to."

"That's *never* going to happen. This sucks," she complains.

"Hate to butt in, but you built the house before you found Christy and the girls," I correct.

"Mommy, can Daddy take us for ice cream?" Harper asks.

"Or maybe Uncle Maddux!" Ry chimes in.

It's only been days, but I love these little girls. I may not want to settle down myself, but I'm digging being the cool uncle. It's fun to load them up on sugar and send them back home with Ryan. I'm getting him back for all the times he annoyed the crap out of me growing up.

Ryan scoops one of his daughters up into his arms. "I wish I could, but Uncle Maddux and I have to head out here soon."

The two of them wrinkle their noses in disappointment and scurry down the hall to their iPad in the front room. Soon after, we hear the sweet sounds of their twin gibberish and laughter.

"Seriously? But we're not done packing." Christy puffs out her lower lip.

From the way Ryan lowers his eyes to that pout, I can tell he's gonna make her "pay" for it when he gets home later.

I look back at Brooks.

She's watching me with an expression I can't read.

I'm not quite sure what I did to deserve that look. It's almost an accusation. *Did I say something to offend her? Maybe I wasn't supposed to touch the tarot cards. Perhaps it's some sort of superstition.*

But how could I have known?

I was just joking.

Is that it? Did I offend her? I can't get a read on her. But something about the way her hand felt on my chest when she lost her balance ignited something in me. I feel drawn to her.

"I know, baby, but Maddux and I have had this planned for days. It's card night with the boys, you know."

Christy huffs. "Fine."

"So, someone likes cards, huh?" Brooks mumbles.

I turn my attention back to her. She spoke to me. *Finally.* That's much different from the usual cold shoulder she gives me, like she'd do anything to avoid me. But she seems like that with everyone. Very standoffish and not at all friendly.

"Only the kinds I can win at." I flash her a grin, trying to show her I'm unphased, but that's a lie.

"Come on, man. We need to get going or we're gonna be late." Ryan grabs Christy by the waist and covers her mouth hungrily with his own.

I can't help but steal another glance at Brooks. She's watching them with a weird sadness in her eyes that I can't quite place. *Maybe she's just sad that her best friend is moving out. Is Christy her only friend?*

Ryan clasps a hand on my shoulder and steps past me into the hall. The twins barrel into him.

I pause behind him, right beside a door I haven't seen open before. I swear it was closed moments ago.

I spy a large, queen-sized bed, black silk sheets, and a heavy, dark blue comforter that looks pretty inviting right now.

What I wouldn't give to slide her body under them and have my way with her...

Flanking each side of the bed, two nightstands hold lamps, candles, books, and… I blink not believing my eyes.

I turn back toward Brooks, who is still standing near the doorway of Christy and the twins' room. Her green eyes meet mine, and for just a second, I feel like I see the same want…the same need…reflected back at me.

Yep.

One day, Brooks.

One day.

12

NO-CONTACT RULE

Brooks

My throat's tight, and my chest feels heavy. I can't breathe, and my eyes are having a hard time focusing. *It doesn't usually work this way.*

I don't think it's possible.

For all my life, whenever I touch someone, I see them—their past and their future. Like with Christy, I saw Ryan coming before she did. I knew my best friend would find happiness. But it isn't always as pleasant. I see things I don't always want to see. I avoid contact; I hate touch.

My no-contact rule has extended into adulthood, much to my dismay. I've never had a relationship with anyone—never known a man's touch.

Maddux...

I didn't *see* anything when I touched him. For just one moment, I was able to lose myself in the closeness, in his warmth, in the strength I felt beneath his blue button-down shirt that electrified his blue eyes. *What I wouldn't give to feel his arms wrap around me, pull me tight against his hardness, and slide me along his length.*

Christy is rambling away and shoving miscellaneous items into boxes. She's lost in her own world, barely needing any acknowledgement from me except a slight nod and a mumbled "uh-huh" at the appropriate times. Which means I can get absorbed in my own thoughts.

Of Maddux.

Maddux... Really? Of all people.

Why'd it have to be him? Just my luck that it couldn't have been with someone I actually liked, someone I actually had something in common with.

He doesn't even have tattoos.

He's a tattoo virgin.

I look down at my arms and legs, which are covered in sharp lines and expert shading. *We're definitely opposites.*

But opposites are supposed to attract, and I'm definitely attracted to Maddux.

Gross.

No, I'm not.

He's arrogant. He's everything I'm not and never want to be. Maddux belongs to a country club. He has guys' poker nights with the same group of frat-type boys I've avoided my entire life. Maddux is everything my parents would want for me...and everything I've never desired for myself.

Until now.

"Earth to space cadet. Come in, Brooks." Christy waves a hand in front of my face. "Where were you just now?"

"Right here, listening to you drone on and on about how happy you are to move out of this cramped apartment and into that huge mansion lover boy's built for his large family." I roll my eyes with faux exaggeration and shoot her a smile.

"I so was not! In fact, I dread it." Christy slumps onto her bed with a huff. "What if things don't work out?"

"Oh, come on—"

"No, Brooks, I'm serious. What if the girls and I move in with Ryan and he decides it's too much?" The look she gives me is hopeful yet terrified.

"I don't think you're being fair to Ryan. He seems like a perfectly nice guy that dotes on you and the twins." Her hand is trembling, and I want to take it, tell her everything is going to work out, but I can't. She knows why. Instead, I say, "You and the girls will always have a home here with me." I would love to hug her right now. "But you need to trust me. Happily ever after." I tap my temple, reminding her I've seen it all play out in my visions.

Christy nods and wipes a lingering tear from her cheek. "Thank you. I'm just so overwhelmed by all of this. It seems like it's all happening all of a sudden."

"That's not true," I argue.

"No?"

"Christy, you've been taking care of that man's twin girls for almost six years by yourself. No, I don't think that their father coming back and taking care of you and them is in any way 'all of a sudden.'" I even use air quotes for emphasis.

She doesn't understand how lucky she is. All I have is my work.

Which reminds me…

"But as much as I want to help you continue packing, I need to hop in the shower and get ready for work. I'm already running late as it is."

"You're the owner. You can go in any time you want…and take off any time you want," Christy adds with a wink, gesturing toward the stack of empty boxes in the corner of her bedroom.

I shake my head. "Not a chance, bestie. You have fun with this. I need a snack and a shower."

13

SCREAM HIS NAME

Brooks

The kitchen in my home is a mess of boxes and scattered packing materials. The only things left out are two pints of ice cream, plastic utensils, a mostly empty bottle of chardonnay, and two barstools. Christy's hair is wrapped in an old bandana I've seen her wear throughout the years of our friendship whenever she stress-cleans.

I slump on a barstool, swiveling it slightly on squeaky hinges with a sigh of my own. My slender fingers wrap around the container of rich chocolate and peanut butter ice cream—nothing but the best for our girl talks. Leaning on the counter, her chin draped lazily over one propped arm, Christy digs into her own pint, a mix of frustration and exhaustion etched across her face.

"I can't believe I have to unpack all of this," Christy groans, gesturing toward the chaos surrounding them. "I never realized I had this many things. Moving with the twins is going to be the death of me."

"Ryan can afford movers to do all of this," I motion around the apartment with my hands.

She shakes her head.

"You could always throw it away," I suggest.

"What? No. I could never. I still remember purchasing half of this stuff. The twins and I acquired so much together with you. I know Ryan can afford to buy me newer things, nicer things, but I just don't think I could part with all these memories."

I smile. "And this is why you're my best friend." With a nod of sympathy, my layered black hair falling over one eye, I tilt my head and look down at my pint of ice cream. "I can only imagine how hard this is for you, moving away from the only home the twins have ever known. But think of it this way…you're moving into Ryan's mansion. You're with the man you love after all these years without him. It'll be like a fresh start—a beautiful home for you and the girls. One the three of you more than deserve."

I long to reach forward and grasp Christy's arm lightly with a gentle squeeze.

Christy rolls her eyes and takes another spoonful of ice cream. "It's a house, not a mansion," she corrects. "Don't remind me about all of the responsibilities that will come with that. I'm not sure I'm ready for it all."

"What do you mean?"

"You know, all the country club nonsense. I think all of it's kind of silly."

"At least you'll have some good gossip to share on our lunch dates," I say with a giggle.

"Touché!" Christy turns to place her spoon in the trash then puts the rest of her pint of ice cream in the freezer.

I understand Christy's dilemma, but at the same time, a small part of me is looking forward to having my apartment all to myself for the first time.

When Christy turns back from the sink, she has a mischievous glint to her eye.

I pause, spoon halfway to my mouth. "What?"

"So…I was wondering…"

"No." I shake my head adamantly.

"No? You didn't even let me finish what I was going to say!" Christy objects.

"I don't have to. Anytime you start out a sentence like that, it's always some sort of shenanigans that I don't want any part of."

Christy sticks her bottom lip out in a pout I'm sure Ryan finds absolutely impossible to resist. I shake my head again.

"Nuh-uh. That's not going to work. I resist!"

"Oh, come on! That's not fair. It wasn't anything bad. I promise."

"You promise?" I raise an eyebrow.

"Yes!"

"You promise, and you swear it?"

"*Yes!*"

"Okay," I relent. "Lay it on me."

"I was just wondering what was going on with you and Maddux..." Christy mumbles.

Damn it! My mouth falls open, and I roll my eyes.

"Is that your way of telling me there's nothing going on there? No sparks?" Christy narrows her eyes.

"Why would you even think that?"

Christy shrugs. "I don't know. I see the way he looks at you. There definitely seems to be some interest, at least on his end."

I try to quell the butterflies in my stomach.

Nope. Not going to do this.

These butterflies need to stop. There's nothing between Maddux and me. He's a player, and I have taste. Yes, he's ungodly handsome, and I'm sure he could do a great number of amazing things to my body. But he's probably done those same things to every woman in this city. I don't want any part of that.

When I glance up at Christy, she's looking at me knowingly. *A part of her probably already knew the answer before she asked the question. After all, she is my best friend. She knows me better than I know myself.*

Instead of being honest, I do my best to appear nonchalant, determined not to let my attraction to Maddux get the better of me.

His brooding demeanor and piercing blue eyes...the air of mystery that draws me in... It's the equivalent of wanting something simply because I can't have it. The heartache and the pain he would cause me just wouldn't be worth it.

But the sex... Oh, the sex would definitely be worth it.

"Nah," I reply casually, taking another bite of my ice cream.

"Maddux and I are just friends because of Ryan and you... Acquaintances. Nothing more."

Christy seems unconvinced. "Are you sure about that? There's something in the way he looks at you, Brookie..."

I love that she calls me that. I detest my first name. It is a constant reminder of my mother and her maiden name.

"And I'm sure I'm not the only one he looks at like that. You're probably just mistaking his undress-me-eyes for something else. It isn't what you think."

"Okay. If you say so." Christy winks. "I need to use the bathroom. I'll be right back."

When Christy leaves the room, I feel my resolve crashing around me. My mind races with the conflicting thoughts that have been bombarding me since I last saw Maddux here, in my house, in my tattoo parlor downstairs. I can't bury them. I can't ignore them. I can't forget him.

Maddux.

I wonder what it would be like to scream his name while he's buried deep inside me...

No.

I'm not going to go there.

I can't go there. I have to maintain my self-restraint; otherwise, whatever he's stirring inside me is going to become even more obvious to everyone else around me.

Around us.

And what would that mean for Maddox?

I'm not sure he'd want to be associated with someone like me, someone completely not part of his perfectly put-together world.

Even though his brother is marrying my best friend.

But with me, it's different.

I know that.

And he knows that.

Right?

Christy is right. He does look at me with something like hunger in his eyes...something like need. Each time, it stirs a warmth in my core.

I'm just not sure how much longer I can pretend I don't want him, too...

The coolness of the water hitting my skin does nothing to quell the warmth growing in me. I thought a quick shower would erase all thoughts of Maddux and allow me to go to work with a clear head, but I'm not having much luck with that.

How am I going to tattoo anyone like this, when all I can see is the look on his face when my hand landed on his chest?

The answer? I'm not. I need to find a way to wash him from my thoughts. Every time I close my eyes... I see him, his smile, his hair, his muscles, and his dimple.

Please...

Please... Anyone but Maddux.

14

LET'S ROB THEM

Maddux

"Yo, Maddux, get your head in the game."

I look across the table at Ryan, surprised he hasn't kicked me under the table by now. No, my head hasn't been in the game. It's been on Brooks.

Which is absurd. I can't stand her, and she obviously can't stand me. Every time I see her, it's like a battle of wits, and I'm somehow always losing. It wasn't attractive until today.

I shake my head, trying to clear it.

I'm not going to win like this.

The two men at the table with us are older. They're corporate CEOs with money to burn. Obviously...or they wouldn't be here. *The same men who scoff at department store Santa's ringing the bell for spare change, who shut their doors in Girl Scouts' faces, who haven't donated blood or money to anything greater than themselves...ever.*

And now, I'm going to rob them.

No, I don't mean like that. I don't believe in firearms or violence.

I'm doing it the old-fashioned way.

Poker.

From my periphery, I glance at Wade, Steve, and Roberto at the other tables. Everyone appears calm, collected. No one around us seems to suspect anything.

And why would they? Willie arranged this poker night. He's the best of the best, and he's on our side. He knows who to invite, who has the deepest pockets, and who won't ever go public, no matter what they lose. Willie organizes underground poker games with a large buy-in and even more potential for winnings. We're talking in the tens of thousands each hand.

What we're doing is dangerous. These are powerful men in their own rights. *They might not go to the police if they find out what we're doing, but they'll find other ways to get even.*

And yet we rob from the rich and give to those who need it.

I replay the pickleball game a year ago that started it all.

"You know what I don't understand?"

We all turned to Wade. He's soft-spoken and not easily angered, but that day, something was different.

He took a deep breath before continuing. "Why do we spend so much time here?" Wade gestured toward the couples playing tennis on the court beside us and the sea of luxury cars in the parking lot beyond it.

"What do you mean?" Roberto asked, wiping the sweat from his face with a towel then slinging it over his shoulder. "What else would you rather be doing?"

"That's not what I mean, and you know it."

Willie and I shared a look then turned to Wade. He sighed.

"Don't you guys wish you could make a difference? Do something? Be a part of something? Maddux, look at you. You worked your butts off to get to where you are, right?"

I chuckled. "I mean, I like to think so. It certainly wasn't handed to me."

"That's what I mean!" Wade raised a hand in the air and gestured wildly toward me. "That's what I mean. You worked your. butt off, and you made millions in real estate. How anyone can pull that off is beyond me, but you did it! Roberto, same for you. And Willie... Well, I don't really know what the hell you do. But none of us come from old family money. And look at each of you—you're more generous than any old sandbagger here. Some of these men are billionaires. And they'd rather spit on others than lend a helping hand."

"What's gotten into you?" I asked.

Willie and Steve looked as confused as I was.

Wade sighed. "I stopped for a coffee after the gym this morning. I needed a pick-me-up after the redhead I took home last night. She did a number on me. And what she can do with... But you guys don't wanna hear about that—"

"Like hell we don't," Roberto objected.

Willie groaned.

"Later, man. We'll talk about it over lunch. But anyway, I saw an older dude walk out the café before me. Recognized him as some big shot with a membership from here. Don't know his name. Don't know anything else about him, really. But there was this woman... She was obviously homeless. Her clothes were nothing but rags, and she was real dirty. But she smiled. She actually smiled at this man and asked him to buy her a sandwich. Dude, she wanted a sandwich—not spare change, not a few bucks. All she wanted was a sandwich because she was hungry, and the man pushed past her. Didn't even have the courtesy to walk around. I just...I can't...I don't want to be like that. I want to do better. Be better."

Willie shrugged. "Then let's do it."

"But how?" I asked. "We can't really get a bunch of old men to change who they are. We're no one to them. Not like we're gonna have any sort of influence."

Roberto smiled and clasped my shoulder. "Let's just rob them."

"Yeah. Okay." I smiled but noticed Willie wasn't chuckling like the rest.

"No, let's do that," he mumbled almost incoherently.

"Willie, are you listening to yourself?" I was sure he wasn't serious.

"Leave it to me." With that, he threw his racket to Wade and walked away.

And that's how our scheme was born.

Over the next few months, Willie gathered everything we needed to pull it off without being detected. One of his contacts—none of us knows who—supplies the cards for each game. They appear sealed, brand new, never been used. But each card is actually marked with ink that's only visible under blue light.

Each of us wears either glasses or contacts with a special film that allows us to see the ink. The best part is that ordinary glasses and contacts can't detect it. And the lights in the room don't pick up the ink. *It's flawless.*

So far, we've won millions. It's pocket change to these men we're taking it from. They'll never miss it. Each of them will find a way to write it off for a tax break, lie to their wives, and pretend the new necklace they bought was more expensive than it actually was. Maybe they'll get a little upset for losing so much money to us. *I'd call that a win-win.*

With the money, we do what these men should have done with it all along.

We donate it to charities; we help people who really need it.

I'm not doing as well tonight as I usually do. My mind is full of other things.

Brooks.

That damn girl. What am I thinking?

It will never work.

"Maddux? You in for another hand?"

If anyone would understand this struggle, Ryan would. He knows Christy and Brooks better than I do. But I can't talk to him.

Not about this.

"Nah. I think I need to head out. I have a headache, and it's breaking my concentration. I'm going to call it a night."

No, I'm not. I need to get laid.

Sleep isn't on the menu.

At another table, Roberto and Steve both shoot me questioning glances, but I'm sure Ryan will fill them in later. These games have another three hours to go.

There's no way I can last that long.

I need to get her off my mind.

"Don't take too much of his money." I lean toward the older gentleman to my right and indicate my head toward my partner in crime, Wade, trying to hold my breath against the smoke from the man's cigar.

I know full well Wade will take him for everything he has. The old man doesn't stand a chance.

I'm grateful Ryan drove himself tonight. It saves me having to take him home.

As I walk out the door, shrugging on my jacket, I pull my phone from my pocket. *Which app will it be tonight?*

Better yet, how can I possibly get a black-haired, green-eyed beauty out of my mind and into my bed?

15

THIS ISN'T ME

Maddux

This woman does not disappoint.

Her dark blue Ford Fusion was waiting in front of my usual hotel by the time I pulled up. *I wonder what it says about me that I have a normal hotel for this sort of thing.* It's certainly not a five-star hotel. I don't consider my random hook-ups to be worth all of that, though I definitely could afford it. The place is nice, and it's clean.

She knows who I am, and I'm okay with that. *What's she going to say? It's not like I'm paying her.* I'm known in my circles for being somewhat of a playboy, so these sort of meetups are expected. *Needed.* My job is stressful, the poker games even more so.

I know what she's thinking while she's with me. She's thinking that if she does everything just right…if she does everything I like …then I'll be more apt to see her again, maybe take her out on a real date. That there might be a future here.

But I'm not having that.
Not with this one.
Not with anyone.

Brooks.

This girl's a blonde, but that's not what I see. When I blink, her blue eyes seem emerald; the golden tangles clenched in my hand flash black. Instead of a black party dress draped over the chair beside us, I picture a certain plaid skirt, a T-shirt with some rock band I've never heard of, and fishnet, thigh-high stockings.

No… The fishnets would stay on.

The blonde—*what was her name again? Abby? Amanda? Ugh…I'm a dick.*

I attempt to be in the moment. I try to concentrate on the sensations…

Brooks.

Why am I thinking about her right now? It almost throws me off.

What is happening to me?

Man up, Maddux. This isn't like you. This isn't who you are. You don't catch feelings for people. You have one-night stands. That's all you do.

Brooks wouldn't fit into my world. Her style?

Yeah, it's pretty damn hot. She's certainly gotten my attention. But that's not all I'm thinking about, is it?

No. For some reason, I'm picturing cookouts with her, Christy, and Ryan, or taking her to eat at the country club.

Taking her out for a nice dinner, and then to my house afterward.

At my house?

What am I thinking?

I never take women to my house.

This isn't like me.

But this chick isn't doing it for me.

It feels good, but it doesn't feel like it's enough.

Not this time.

Why?

For the first time, I have to stop myself from saying someone's name.

Brooks.

16

WORTH IT?

Maddux

"You up for a tattoo?" Ashley—no, Amber—asks. *Why can't I remember her name?*

"Come again?" I look at her, my brow furrowed, confused.

I'm normally not awkward at this point in a hookup. Usually, we just get dressed, say our goodbyes, and go our separate ways. I never ask for phone numbers, never arrange a second meeting. None of them have ever impressed me that much.

Why is this one still here?

"You know, the night is still young, and I want a tattoo. I heard there's this cool little shop downtown. I think it's owned by some rocker-type chick."

She must be mistaking my shocked expression for contemplation because she continues.

"You don't have to get one, of course. I just thought it might be cool to get out, not have to go home so early. Besides, you might like me the more you get to know me."

She follows it with a wink, and I have to bite my tongue to keep from telling her that she looks ridiculous with her smudged mascara.

No, I won't like her the more I get to know her.

I already know that.

What are the odds of there being another tattoo shop run by a "rocker-type chick"? She has to be talking about Brooks's shop.

And I'd love to see her right now.

Brooks is aware of me. I saw it in her eyes earlier. *Whatever passed between us, she felt it, too.*

She's not going to make this easy.

But if I have her—no, when I have her—I can't treat her like one of my usuals. That crap won't fly with Christy or Ryan.

This time, it's gotta be different.

But do I really want that?

Is it worth it?

17

DELICIOUS V

Brooks

You've got to be kidding me. Not today. Not after what happened. I can't believe he has the nerve to show up here…with her…

Maddux.

And who is with him?

She looks a little rough. Not his usual type. Though, I'm not really sure what his type actually is.

I raise an eyebrow.

"Welcome to Ink, Inc. Take a look around," I say in my usual cheery tone.

No sense acting like I know him. It's the second time he's been in my tattoo parlor but the first time I'm seeing him with this blonde woman. *I'm not sure how I feel about it. This feels a little like jealousy.*

Seriously? Jealousy? Over Maddux?

That's gross.

Is it really?

The light blue V-neck T-shirt he's wearing stretches tightly over his pecs, the same firm ones I collided with earlier. It tapers down toward his six-pack, and when he shifts from side to side, I can almost see the thin material getting caught in the ridges.

I bet he has a delicious V leading down toward...

Never mind.

I can't think about that right now and maintain my composure. *Evidently, my shower time wasn't enough to get Maddux out of my mind.*

He smiles, flashing that solitary dimple, and my body betrays me.

How does he keep doing this to me?

For some reason, Maddux isn't taking his eyes off me. And he's not shy about it. He's not even trying to hide it.

Maddux bites his bottom lip a little bit. He lifts his eyes back to mine—*those gorgeous blue eyes of his*—and then drops them down to the purple and black plaid skirt I chose to wear to work.

I bet he likes what he sees.

I should walk across the room with a little extra sway in my hips.

Nope.

Oh, my God.

Nope.

I turn back to my client. Thankfully, I'm almost finished. The soft whir of the tattoo gun is comforting, almost hypnotic, and I can almost drown out the conversation he's having with the unkempt blonde.

Almost...

"What should I get?" Her voice is a little whiny, not something I could listen to for long periods of time.

"I don't know. It's your body and your tattoo."

"Yeah, but I want it to be sexy. Like me."

Oh man, this can't get any worse.

She laughs, and it's like nails on a chalkboard.

I was wrong. It can definitely get worse.

Thankfully, Maddux doesn't reply.

The blonde circles around to the wall closest to my station. Her perfume is nauseating, and my client looks uncomfortable.

You're not the only one, buddy.

I wipe off the last of the excess ink. "There you go, David. All done."

"Wow, Brooks. This looks amazing. Exactly what I wanted. You're so damn talented. I did the right thing by coming to you instead of going to that crap hole down the street," he says, admiring the new addition to his sleeve.

Before I can speak, the blonde chimes in. "Eh. It's not something I'd get, but it looks all right."

David and I turn to her in shock, and Maddux looks mortified at her side.

I have to stifle a giggle at his expression. *This is definitely something I can work with.*

"So, Maddux, are you gonna introduce me to your friend?" I take off my outer pair of gloves and begin cleaning up my station, but I pause for a quick glance at his face.

His cheeks are flushed, and he's looking at the blonde with a slight, fish-mouthed "O."

Oh, this is even better than I thought. Maddux doesn't even know the blonde's name.

"Oh, um," he stutters. "This is…my friend…"

She looks at him expectantly.

No, honey, you weren't special. You're just like all the others he's had in his bed before you. I'd find it funny if I didn't suddenly feel sort of sad for her. Any hope she had of turning this obvious hook-up into something more is slowly draining out of her eyes.

Poor thing.

"My name is Abbey, asshole."

She turns and storms out of the shop. The little bell above the front door is almost deafening in the silence left in her wake.

Maddux turns back to me, his lips pursed. "Damn, that was awkward."

"You didn't remember her name? Really? That's low," I say with a slight snicker. I might feel bad for the blonde…Abbey…but watching Maddux squirm is still a great deal of fun.

"Yeah. Well, I didn't really expect for the night to continue as long as it did." He crosses his arms over his chest, and his already large biceps clench. The veins stick out along his tanned forearms.

My core heats up…*again*. I lick my lips, and his eyes dart to my mouth then back up to my eyes.

Nope. I imagined it.
I'm reading too much into it.
There's nothing between us.
But I want there to be, don't I?

"You know, Maddux, I kinda agree with her. You are kinda an asshole."

I turn away from him, hoping he won't notice the blush building up on my cheeks, the sudden perspiration at the thought of him with me.

Because I want nothing more at this moment.

I'm finding it very hard to resist Maddux when I really want to hate him.

18

THAT NAME AGAIN

Maddux

I lean back and let the early afternoon sun warm my face. My gaze drifts across the meticulously manicured backyard lining my custom pool. The edges are beveled with luminescent stones, and the interior is lined with a pearly blue tile, giving the water a vivid cerulean tinge.

I kick my feet in the warm water, making sure to keep the bottom edges of my khaki shorts from getting wet. My hair ruffles in the gentle breeze, and I let out a deep sigh.

My thoughts wander to Brooks.

Hot-as-hell Brooks with her short plaid skirts and fishnet stockings…

Just the memory of the last time I saw her is enough to make my pants uncomfortable.

When my phone buzzes, I almost groan at the interruption.

"Ugh," I mumble. "What do you want, little brother?"

"Nice to hear from you, too, bro. Whatcha up to?"

"Relaxing by the pool."

"In your bright pink speedo?" Ryan chuckles on the other end of the line.

"Only in your dreams. What can I do you for?"

"You up for helping me put some furniture together?" Ryan's voice almost sounds apologetic. He knows how much I hate doing stuff like this.

"Seriously? Why don't you just buy the good stuff? You know, the furniture that comes with the white-glove delivery?"

Ryan lets out an exasperated sigh. "I knoooow. I tried to tell Christy that, but she had her heart set on these particular bunk beds. And wouldn't you know? It comes in about 200 little pieces that are scattered all over my living room right now."

"Ugh." I cringe and rub my eyes.

"Please?"

"Only if you stop whining. And you owe me a drink. Maybe drinks, plural, depending on whether or not the directions are decipherable."

"You're a lifesaver," Ryan says with a sigh.

"See you in five."

Ryan's house is just down the street from mine, but I purposefully take my time. There are a lot of things I can imagine doing with my afternoon, but this isn't high on the list.

He greets me at the door with a cold beer—my consolation prize, I suppose.

"Thanks for coming. It would have taken me all night to get this thing together otherwise. And you know Christy and the girls want to sleep in it tonight."

I laugh. I'd agree with him, but I don't really know.

"Speaking of your better half, are Christy and the twins here?"

"Nah. They're at Brooks's."

Brooks.

There's that name again.

I'm never going to escape it—or her. The only way through this is to just get it over with and sleep with her.

Another time, Maddux. Another time.

Time to switch the topic to something safer.

I settle on the living room floor across from Ryan, the piles of boards, nuts, and bolts between us.

"Oh boy. You weren't kidding…"

"I know." He groans. "This is the last time I let her buy furniture. I'm putting my foot down."

"Uh-huh. I bet," I reply with a wink.

I may not know much about women, but I know he's full of crap if he thinks Christy's ever going to let him wear the pants in this relationship. Ryan might as well kiss his black credit card goodbye.

"Any idea how much you won last night?" my brother inquires, not knowing the real reason I attended.

The private poker game went off without a hitch from what I've gathered so far, but I still need a grand total from my crew in order to plan what charities I'll be funding this month.

"I won over $300,000," Ryan shares.

"Damn. That's not bad at all. Great job. I'm sorry I couldn't stick around."

"No problem. You're making up for it now." Ryan looks up at me and laughs.

As much as I hate putting furniture together, I love spending time with my little brother. I feel like we don't do enough of this, but now that he's becoming a family man, I'm sure there will be more holiday dinners and celebrations. *I just hope I don't feel out of place as the cool bachelor uncle without a family of my own.*

And I'm sure Brooks will be there. She's Christy's family.

"So, I see you've got a thing for Brooks."

I feel the color drain from my face. "Excuse me?"

"Hey. Don't deny it. I noticed you giving Brooks the side eye. And I know how you are."

"What's that supposed to mean?" I look at him, feeling anger flare in my chest, but I know his next words are completely justified.

"I know you like the frequent company of women; that's all. You aren't really the settle-down type."

He's right. I'm not. Yet something about Brooks makes me question myself.

"Yeah... She seems cool and all. But she isn't really my type. And like you said, I'm not looking for a wifey right now. I have too much going on." I attempt to validate my bachelor ways.

Ryan nods, concentrating more on the screw he's driving home than my words.

But my internal grumbling is interrupted by the sound of the garage door opening.

I look at Ryan and raise a brow.

That voice. The sweet tinkle of melodic laughter.

Her.

This feels like an ambush.

"Are you serious?" I hiss, trying to keep my voice low.

"What?" Ryan whispers back harshly.

"You didn't tell me *she* was going to be here. Did you do this on purpose?"

"No," he laughs.

"No, what?" Christy asks, coming around the corner from the mudroom, followed by Brooks.

"Nothing, baby." Ryan shoots me a warning glance.

But I barely register it. Brooks's body is covered by nothing more than a swath of fabric posing as a blue plaid skirt, and all I can think about is everything I'd like to do with her.

My heart stutters, and I swear I spot a faint flush creep up Brooks's chest and neck.

Does she know what she does to me?

Do I affect her when she sees me?

Christy leans down and kisses Ryan on the forehead. He looks at her with so much love in his eyes that I simultaneously want to vomit and search Brooks's eyes for some trace of what I'm feeling.

This is new. She's not like the others.

I have to keep my distance.

I can't allow myself to fall for her.

Brooks and I have trouble written all over us.

19

WHO'S THE LUCKY LADY?

Maddux

Ryan and I sit on the back porch. I'm drinking my fifth and he's on his second beer of the day, and we're basking in the glory of having finished what was quite a harrowing project, with multiple curses and smashed thumbs.

"I still can't believe you," I say low, so the women won't hear.

"That I asked you to help me put the bunk beds together?"

"That you tried to play matchmaker."

He coughs and tries to play it off like he's clearing his throat. "I don't know what you're talking about."

"Ryan, she's not my type. You know that. What if I showed up at the country club fundraiser with her? Can you imagine what everyone would think? How would that look for my company? For your charities? I have to maintain my image."

He rolls his eyes.

"What?" I ask, finding my temper flaring.

"All I'm hearing are excuses and crutches. You're too scared to take a chance. I get it. My older brother's a pussy. I won't let your secret get out."

I groan. "It would definitely give *The Back 9 Talk* something to post."

Christy walks up behind us and drapes herself casually over Ryan's shoulders. "Ugh. That rumor blog? Why are you two discussing that site? I didn't think gossiping was your thing, babe."

"It wasn't me!" Ryan objects, making room on his lap for his woman. "Maddux over here seems to think that whoever runs the blog is going to be super concerned about his dating life."

Christy looks up quickly. "Dating life? Who's the lucky lady?"

She quickly flicks her eyes toward Brooks, hoping I stay far from her best friend.

Don't worry; I don't plan on dating your best friend.

But part of me wants to look at her... to see her reaction. *What would she think if I did start dating someone else? Would she be jealous?*

I casually shake my head with a quick shrug. "I don't know what you guys are talking about. I'm not dating anyone anytime soon. We were just talking about *The Back 9 Talk* and how they're overly interested in everyone's private lives."

"Everyone's private lives," Christy says with a giggle. "Not just the overly snobby types at the club."

Brooks shifts in the Adirondack chair beside me. I can barely breathe, let alone think. What this woman does to me is excruciating.

But I have to play it cool.

Christy shrugs. "Not like any of us can do anything about that. But what you *can* do something about is the boxes still in my trunk..."

Ryan groans. "Seriously, babe? We just spent all afternoon on these damn bunk beds."

"That I am so thankful for." She kisses the corner of his mouth.

"Good. So, can't the boxes wait until tomorrow?"

Christy leans down, her lips are lightly brushing against Ryan's ear and whispers something low. When I see Ryan shifting in his seat, I know I'm doomed to unload these boxes.

He suddenly jumps to his feet and throws Christy over his shoulder. She squeals in delight.

"We'll be right back."

When they disappear inside the house, I turn to Brooks. She's holding her cup of soda to her lips, glancing at me over the rim of it, her dark lashes lowered.

Gah, she's stunning.

And Ryan's just given me a lot of ideas I'd like to do with her.

Will we ever reach that point? Will I ever be able to touch her freely?

"Looks like we're stuck on box duty, huh?"

"It looks like it." Brooks stands and smooths her short skirt.

Out of nervousness?

If anyone should be nervous, it's me. I stand to lose the most here.

Right?

But how much do I stand to gain?

Brooks cautiously steps into the house, but whatever Ryan and Christy are doing, it's nowhere near us. I follow behind her, wanting to put my hand on her lower back and guide her into a room of our own.

Stop it, Maddux.

Now's not the time.

Boxes. We need to bring in these boxes. Then, I need to get the hell out of here and go home.

That isn't helping.

"There aren't too many. And none of them are very heavy. I helped her load them myself," she says with a smile, and I feel tension draining from my shoulders.

"Sounds good," I reply nonchalantly.

But that isn't what I want to say to her. I want to start a conversation. I want to know more about her.

The Back 9 Talk.

I have to remind myself what a rumor blog would do to my business, to my standing in the community, if I'm caught dating someone like Brooks. *She doesn't fit into my world, into my lifestyle.*

A tattoo artist? No way. They'd laugh me out of the country club, and then I'd never have the opportunity to earn what I do for the charities I'm involved with.

I can't risk that, even for someone as fine as Brooks.

"Let's get these boxes inside."

20
I'M HUNGRY

Brooks

It's been almost an hour, and Ryan and Christy are showing no signs of surfacing. I don't blame them. Maybe if I knew what sex was like, I'd understand.

But I don't...

The life of a virgin. A perpetual virgin, at the rate I'm going. My gift has kept me from any physical contact, and it's killing me. I've told myself I'm okay with it, that I can go the rest of my life without the touch of another human, but the more time I spend with Maddux, the crazier I think I am for that.

The fact he doesn't give me visions... I can't deny that I want him.

But he isn't good for me.

Am I so sure that I even want something good for me, though? Wouldn't the bad boy be better? At least, that's what I've read in the spicy romance novels I keep on my bedside tables.

I have toys, but I know it's not the same.

I'm sure Maddux could show me things I'd never...

I sigh. *It's useless. My life has never been on the trajectory to happily ever after like my bestie's. It's why I'm as independent as I am. Being able to know everyone's past, present, and future with a simple touch never changed my life for the better. And I don't expect it to make any allowances for me now.*

Maddux sits on the couch across the room from me, but I wonder what we're waiting for. *Are we hoping Ryan and Christy come out so we can say our goodbyes? Or are we hoping the other person will speak, make a move, do something to progress whatever is building between us?*

Looking at him, I'm almost certain that he feels the same way. At the very least, there's a sexual tension making the air between us heavy with anticipation.

With need.

I want this.

Does he?

Maddux looks up at me, almost as if he hears my thoughts. He clears his throat. "I'm hungry."

"Umm," I say, trying to sound casual and half interested.

"I'm craving a greasy burger at the club." There's something like hope shining in his eyes. I don't know if he's inviting me to join him.

Surely, he won't see me like that.

"They will be busy for at least an hour. Trust me," he states.

I shouldn't trust him. Not with my heart, not with my body, not with anything.

His eyes linger on mine then drop to my lips.

Yes, I want that, too. Believe me, Maddux.

"You should probably head out," he informs, pointing to the door.

"I don't have my car here. Christy was my ride." I cringe and shrink inside my fitted T-shirt.

"Hmm..." He pauses to contemplate. "It's Josh's day off, but I'm sure we could find something to eat here." His blue eyes seem like X-ray beams, searching for more than an answer from me.

"Us poor working folk are used to fending for ourselves," I quip, rising from my seat.

I'm acutely aware of his gaze on my backside as we make our way to the kitchen. I open the fridge to find a meat and cheese platter, sandwich fixings, and hamburger patties.

"Wanna grill?" I offer, arching a brow in challenge. "Josh left four hamburger patties and a package of hotdogs. We could grill for everyone, and you said you wanted a burger at the club."

"I'm game if you are," he dares.

Maddux

She's adorable. The sight of Brooks wearing Josh's large apron over her tiny mini-skirt should be hilarious and not alluring. While the front hangs to her knees, the back is an open view of her exposed thighs in her tiny skirt. *I need to distract myself from the view.*

21

JOSH'S APRON NEVER LOOKS SO GOOD

Brooks

"Okay. I've gotta know. How'd you get into the tattoo business? Was it something you'd wanted to do since you were a little girl?" Maddux pries.

I look up, slightly shocked by the question. *Maddux wants to know more about me, about my childhood, about my dreams. Tell me this isn't happening.* Here I am, trying to convince myself I need to keep him at arm's length, while he's trying to figure me out, inquiring on subjects that might open deeper conversations than I think I'm ready to have.

"Umm, I guess I sort of just fell into it. I've always been artistic, but I had a job in high school at a tattoo parlor," I share.

"In high school?" He looks at me incredulously.

"Well, yeah. I wasn't tattooing anyone. I was just helping out around the shop and everything. Little things."

"Bet your parents loved that," Maddux says with a chuckle.

I shake my head. "Nope. Not at all. In fact, I sort of told them I was a barista to keep them off my back."

"Quite the rebel, huh?" There's a mischievous glint in his eyes, and my interest is escalating.

"No... Unfortunately, not really. I was a pretty safe kid. I didn't do much."

"Why not?" He flips the hamburger patties one by one on the grill.

How am I drinking this much soda?

My throat is so parched. I feel like I'm being interrogated.

At least Maddux makes for a hot cop.

Might make for interesting roleplay...

"I didn't have many friends," I reply quietly.

Dangerous territory, Maddux. I don't want to say any more.

"Me neither."

Wow. I wasn't expecting that. Maddux—gorgeous Maddux... How could he not have had many friends?

He must see the questions on my face. "I'm serious. I really didn't. I had Ryan, of course. And he's definitely my best friend now. I don't know what I'd do without him. And I had acquaintances, but no one I really let get close to me."

"I can relate to that," I confess.

"I guess we've all got our secrets, huh?" He almost whispers it, licking his lips in punctuation.

Oh God.

It's a good thing I'm not standing. I feel my knees getting weak, and I'm heating up.

Not good.

Why do I find this man so irresistible?

"I guess we do," I agree.

If he only knew how it felt...how every time I touch someone, I see their past, their present, their future. The good and the bad. Every skeleton in their closest. Every unspoken wish or dream. Every unfulfilled promise. Or how every time I touch him, there is delicious silence. I don't see his every unspoken wish or dream. No unfulfilled promises. Just wonderful silence.

This is what has kept me from having friends, until Christy. Even if I had wanted to keep my distance from her, she wouldn't have let me. Her bubbling personality and complete unwillingness to let me pull away and erect my walls eventually won me over after meeting her during my volunteer time at the home for unwed mothers. Christy had been a resident, pregnant with the twins at that time. After she had them, I wanted them to have a real home, so I invited her to live with me. The rest is history.

Until recently, Christy is the only one—besides my parents—who knows about my abilities, my *gift*.

My curse.

If I invite Maddux into my life, even though I don't *see* anything when I touch him, he'll figure it out eventually. Everyone eventually notices that there's something strange about me.

"Uncle Maddux!" the twins yell, running onto the deck.

"Hi, Miss Brooks," Ry greets with a wave.

"Did you have fun with Gigi?" I ask, relieved I'm no longer alone on the deck with Maddux.

"Where's Mommy and Daddy?" Harper interrupts.

"Right here," Christy announces, Ryan following on her heels.

"Dude." Ryan hits his brother on the back. "You didn't have to grill."

"I couldn't watch Brooks waste away while waiting on the two of you to finish…"

"Little ears," Ryan warns his brother.

Maddux chuckles, amending his comment, "To finish and drive her home."

Across from me Christy blushes.

"Josh's apron has never looked so good," Ryan proclaims, his arm wrapping around my shoulders for a hug.

22

A FULL HOUSE MIGHT COST YOU YOUR FULL HOUSE

Maddux

I read the Sunday rumor post one more time while I wait for my crew to arrive.

The Back 9 Talk—6/25

PSA: A full house might cost you your full house.
Poker with the fellas at the club is one thing; illegal poker rings throughout the metro are costing one member his house in Pyke Place. Recent losses reported over $500,000 were the final straw and have this gambler trying his luck in divorce court.
Rumor has it, he's not the only Lynks at Tryst Falls member participating in these underground games.

"This is a bit out of the way, isn't it?" Willie asks. He flicks the bud of his cigarette and glances at the other men standing in the circle.

"I know, but you know we couldn't risk being seen together anywhere," Wade growls.

I know he's right. I'm frustrated, too. The drive out here was rough—almost two hours one way.

Willie sighs and looks at Roberto, who shrugs.

"Well," Wade begins. "we all saw that post. It has to be Greenberg; he's been drinking at the club and confessing to anyone that will listen. Any clue how this affects us?"

"Yeah. How does Greenberg tie into all of this? He came to some of our games, right?" Steve asks.

Wade nods. "Yeah. We got over a mil from him in the past year."

Willie lets out a whistle. "Whew! Big spenda."

All of us snicker. *Leave it to Willie to ease the tension.*

"From what I've witnessed, it really looks like he just comes to the games and plays. I'm not sure what *The Back 9 Talk* has on him." Steve glances at a pickup truck slowly driving by.

I'm sure we look strange—a group of tall, built men standing on a roadside, like this is some sort of fight club. At least we're giving the locals something to talk about and not The Back 9 Talk.

"I guess that's the million-dollar question. Literally," Roberto says. "What's a stupid rumor blog got on someone like that? How'd they get that information? Who's running it?"

"Scorned wife maybe? Jilted girlfriend?" Willie suggests.

"I don't care who tipped them off. We need to figure out who it is, what they know, and what sort of danger we're all in," Steve notes.

"Exactly," Wade agrees. "If we really took this guy for that much, he's obviously got a lot more. That money can go toward helping a lot of people in this community. It hurts us if he's taken out of the game."

I shrug. "He isn't really being taken out of the game. He's not doing anything. Even if he's under investigation, they wouldn't find anything. He's not involved with us."

"Of course," Willie says, "but he isn't gonna wanna come to poker nights when he's getting this sort of attention. You know that. It's a reputation thing."

I can definitely understand that.

Reputation, that is. Doing things that won't make you look worse than you already think you look.

Brooks.

Is that what I'm doing with her? Hiding from her, avoiding her, turning away from her and the potential I'm recognizing between us?

Possibly.

I know I feel differently toward her and that I'm fighting it.

I was thinking about giving in...

But this situation has brought a lot of feelings to the surface. *If it's this easy for The Back 9 Talk to find out about the poker games, it won't be long before they begin to connect the dots. Right? Isn't that why we're all here? What we're afraid of?*

Can I bring Brooks into my life if this is what I'm risking? I can't tie her to it. It would affect her business, upend everything about her life. And I will always try to shield Ryan from any accountability. What if I can't? What will happen to Christy and the twins? I need to keep Brooks at arm's length, so she can help them through this if something does happen to me.

I don't want to. This feels wrong.

But I know now, more than ever, I need to stop all of this with Brooks before it gets started.

I have to protect her.

23

THINKING ALIKE

Brooks

On the final Friday of June, I rack my brain for how I got myself into this situation.

"Ow! Do you have to pull my hair like that?" I growl.

I've been biting my tongue for the last 30 minutes, but I don't think Christy's any closer to being finished with this curling iron. I agreed to come to her and Ryan's housewarming party as soon as I heard about it—I'll always do everything possible to support my best friend—but when she came up with this idea to do a makeover for the occasion, I was less than enthused.

This isn't me.

But on the other hand, I don't look half bad.

The makeup is more subdued than my normal bright reds and dark eyeliner. Then again, those would look very out of place with this blue sundress she's put me in. Not me at all, not something I'd choose for myself, but I look more like I belong in her new world.

Her country club world.

Wow. When did I make that distinction?

Christy is still the same person I've always known. She likes copious amounts of ketchup on her fries, snores like a freight train, and road rages when someone drives forever with their blinker on without turning. Christy's always running late—I don't think she's been early for an appointment a day in her life. Together, we used to make fun of the same sort of people who are eating hors d'oeuvres and drinking wine in her backyard this evening.

I want this for her. I don't want it to change her. My perception of what she'll want now, what she'll expect, has changed, even if I might be wrong about those assumptions.

She smiles at me in the mirror, and a part of me prays I won't lose my best friend.

"You look stunning. You're seriously going to turn the head of every single guy here today," she gushes, and I can't help but latch onto some of that enthusiasm.

"Yup. When I fall flat on my face in this dress, I'll get *everyone's* attention then," I say jokingly.

I'm thankful she allowed me to choose my own shoes to go with this sundress. I already owned these Rocket Dog platform sandals for special occasions like this.

"Oh, stop. You'll be fine."

Christy pauses for a moment.

"You know, I wonder if *The Back 9 Talk* will be here tonight. Just think... A blog post about this party. Some of these old hags will have to accept me then." She giggles.

I stand up and mentally hug her. "You're the best."

Christy flips her hair, shrugs her shoulders, and beams me a smile. "I know. Now, let's get down there. Just hold my hand so I don't fall down the stairs."

Unlike me, she chose high-heeled wedge sandals.

"You know, single NFL players will be here," she teases.

"Still playing matchmaker, eh?" I say, trying very hard to insert annoyance in my voice.

While I'm sure the guys from Ryan's team will be fine with a capital "F," I must not touch.

It took me all these years to find someone who didn't ignite my clairvoyance. *If I found one person, surely there might be others out there. Right?*

Maybe there's hope for me to have a full, meaningful relationship with someone who wants the same. Because I know Maddux doesn't.

He'll only break my heart.

But I'm going to enjoy him in the meantime, if he offers it again.

The pool patio is decorated with tasteful gray and blue decorations. I love that she tied her favorite color into this introduction to country club society. She's asserting her position among them, that she belongs, that she is a force to be reckoned with. *That's the best friend I know.*

I remain by her side while she plays gracious hostess, all smiles and cheery conversation. *Definitely not my scene.* I prefer to be a wallflower watching from the sidelines, especially in foreign environments like this.

Because while Christy belongs here, on Ryan's arm with everything that entails and everything he can offer her, I don't. I once had enough money in my trust fund for my application to the country club to be approved, but I'd prefer to pretend like I don't even have it. Let them think I'm below them. Let them think I'm out of place. While sometimes society makes me feel like it, I know that I'm not. I chose to use my inheritance from my aunt to buy my business and building outright.

I have a lot to offer.

Christy glances my way as I fight the need to roll my eyes behind a socialite's back, mimicking the dramatic way the woman talks. She can't help but giggle.

There's my best friend.

I'm not going to lose her to this. I've simply gained a brother in Ryan.

A brother with a hot older brother.

An older brother who...

"Thinking about me?" comes a deep voice in my ear, and my core tightens.

Yes. Always yes.

"*Pssh*, no. Not all women are obsessed with you," I retort, but I fear we both know I'm lying.

I'm definitely obsessed with him. *Who wouldn't be?*

"But you are. That's all I need."

I think my heart stopped for a moment there. Or maybe it's my hearing.

Maddux didn't just say that. And if he did, he didn't mean it.

"Don't be silly," I say instead of the numerous other things I could say to show I reciprocate whatever attraction he's feeling.

"Aren't you supposed to remain by Ryan's side to help him this evening?"

"He's a big boy," Maddux assures me.

"What are the two of you whispering about?" Christy asks from my side.

"Nothing," we defend in unison, making ourselves seem guilty.

Frickety. Frick. Frick. Frack! Now we are definitely thinking alike.

24

IT'S TIME

Maddux

I watch her from across the pool.

I can't be obvious about it because there's no telling who is here, watching me, waiting to catch me slipping so they can blast me all over that godforsaken rumor blog. *But no one can fault me for eyeing a gorgeous woman.*

Especially with how she looks today.

Hell, The Back 9 Talk might include her in a post simply because she's the mysterious, stunning woman who graced this party. Who is she? Where did she come from? Who is she sleeping with?

Me. She should be with me.

But it's more than that, isn't it?

Brooks looks at me, blushes, and smiles shyly.

I love it.

At the same time, I'm wondering why she let Christy make her over like this. It's not her. It's not the plaid skirts and fishnets, leather boots and red lipstick I'm used to seeing her in. Those seem much more who she is than this blue wispy sundress and soft curls.

But this way, she fits into my world a hell of a lot easier.

That's selfish, and I know it.

"Whatcha lookin' at, bro?" Ryan says at my shoulder, with a sly grin on his face.

He already knows.

"Stop," I hiss.

"You wound me." He clasps his hand over his check in mock injury.

"Mm-hmm... Whatever you say."

"Enjoying the party?"

"Yeah. Christy and Josh really outdid themselves."

"Have you tried these little quiche things? Man, they're addicting."

I laugh as he shoves a whole one into his mouth with a moan. But when I notice the person staring at me from across the pool, my smile fades immediately.

I nudge Ryan slightly in the elbow. "Is that who I think it is?"

"Huh?" He looks around the patio.

I point with a subtle nod of my head in the man's direction.

"Ohhh... Yeah, that is."

From across the patio, Greenberg's son, Cade, is watching me intently. His penetrating gaze unnerves me. But it dawns on me. *What if Cade is responsible for that The Back 9 Talk blog post about poker? What if Cade's target isn't actually his dad but my guys? What if he's upset that Daddy's blowing his future inheritance, gambling it away, and he is trying to put an end to it?*

What if the young man wants his mil back, and I'm next?

Perhaps the next blog post is already written?

I'm suddenly overcome by this new potential threat, possible backlash on Ryan and his family, and the woman I'd give anything to protect.

"It's time," Ryan informs me.

25

IT'S NOW OR NEVER

Maddux

"Everybody," Ryan calls, hands cupping his mouth. "Can I get everyone's attention, please?"

As the crowd's murmurs cease, Josh pats Ryan on the shoulder before joining Paul. They hold hands in anticipation. Ryan tucks his hands into his shorts' pockets as he begins. "Christy and I would like to thank each of you for joining us tonight to celebrate the new house."

Christy moves to his side while the group claps. In his right pocket, I notice he toys with the box. *It's now or never.*

"And I thought, while I had our closest family and friends as a captive audience, I'd…" He drops to his knee, extending the ring box towards the only woman he has ever loved.

He opens the black velvet box with his left hand as it sits in the palm of his right. The crowd gasps, quietly awaiting Christy's reaction. I watch her eyes tear up as she fans her face. Then she laughs.

"Is this a joke? There's no ring," she says out loud, laughing nervously.

"It is a joke," I loudly announce to my brother's horror.

I whisper in Christy's ear, "Let me say a few words, then you can propose." She nods before I address the crowd.

"The joke is on Ryan," I tell the group, my hands cupping Christy's shoulders from behind.

I look over her, down at my brother still kneeling before her, a devilish grin upon my face.

Together, Christy and I turn from him toward the guests.

"You see, unbeknownst to Ryan, Christy also planned to propose tonight," I explain, and the crowd laughs. "She reached out to me earlier this week for help in getting Ryan's ring size."

That's Christy's cue. She turns towards Ryan, extending her own little black velvet box, opened in his direction as she drops to one knee.

I watch his shock morph to laughter while she waits for Ryan's answer. Instead of an answer, I watch him shake his head no.

"But the joke is also on Christy," I declare, and the crowd erupts.

She peeks into the ring box to find it as empty as Ryan's. In horror, she looks at me. I stand beside her, a devilish grin upon my face.

"Seems these two love birds forgot to ask the two most important people to help." I point to the pool. "Ry and Harper, it's your turn," I announce.

I watch my nieces emerge from the swimming pool, shaking their heads as they approach me. Neither look in the direction of Ryan or Christy. I bend down, allowing the girls a private conference.

"We lost the rings. They fell into the pool. We can't get them." As they talk, their little hands and arms move animatedly until they both point behind them to the swimming pool.

Dumbfounded, I drop to my knees at the edge of the pool, peering into the deep end.

"I've got this," Brooks growls, passing me toward Ryan and Christy. "What is going on?" she asks, loud enough for the guests to hear.

"I...um..." I stammer.

"The rings are down there," the twins announce in unison, pointing to the pool.

Christy gasps, and Ryan wraps his arms around her.

"They are insured," Ryan whispers as a reminder to both of them.

I no longer smile, staring wide-eyed in their direction. One second, my apologetic gaze is on them; the next, I dive headfirst into the swimming pool. I dive over and over, only surfacing when I must for a quick breath.

My mind reels. *I can't believe I trusted five-year-olds with wedding rings. I'm such an idiot.*

26

THE JOKE'S ON YOU

Brooks

"Maddduxxx!" I yell loudly the next time he returns to the surface.

All eyes move to me as I stand at the edge of the pool, the twins hugging my legs and my hands upon my hips.

"You just had to be a prankster," I scold loudly. "You just had to ruin not one but two perfect proposals." I point at him. "Shame on you, Uncle Maddux. I can't believe you would use your little nieces in your evil plan."

I pry the girls' arms from my legs, taking their hands and leading them to Ryan and Christy.

Turning back to Maddux, I ask what we all want to know: "What were you thinking?"

Still treading water in the deep end of the pool, Maddux defends himself. "I thought it would be cute to let the girls hand the two rings to their parents. So, I placed a ring on a safety pin and attached it to each of the girls' swimsuits."

The girls lift the outer leg of their swimsuits, displaying the large safety pins, sans the rings. Then, while Ry leans in to whisper in

Christy's ear, Harper whispers in her father's. They stare, disbelieving what they heard.

"Really?" Ryan asks, and I see Harper nod in my periphery.

"Maybe if a few more adults hop in the pool, we will find the rings on the bottom," Maddux offers, looking at the guests.

Before anyone volunteers, I announce, "That will not be necessary." I bend at the pool's edge, waving for Maddux to approach me. "You see, the joke is on you, Maddux."

The twins jump up and down, cheering, "We got you! We got you, Uncle Maddux!" as they point to him.

"The joke is on you, Uncle Maddux," I barb. "You really thought it prudent to give expensive and important rings to five-and-a-half-year-olds?" I tisk, shaking my head. "What were you thinking?"

"First..." Standing once again, I hold up one finger. "They are little girls." I wave two fingers towards him now. "Second, they are not even six."

Now, as I speak, the girls hold up their own fingers for the group counting.

"Third, your two nieces can't keep a secret," I inform him. "The first time they saw me after you spoke to them, they told me everything. And I mean everything. Like how you originally planned to tie the rings to the suits until Ry asked, 'What if they come untied?' and you then decided to pin them."

I raise my hands and shoulders as if asking what a woman is to do.

"So, when I arrived, I asked the girls to let me hold the rings. I can't believe you didn't even ask to see the rings once in the past four hours." I pause for effect, scanning the crowd.

"When it looked like Josh and Ryan were preparing for the first proposal, I shared a new plan to play a trick on you, Uncle Maddux. And to make sure they kept my secret for 15 minutes, I told them they had to swim until you asked them to climb from the pool."

I stand above Maddux as he sits on the pool's edge. "And that is how you pull off a prank of this magnitude."

The crowd jeers and boos at Maddux.

"Soooo..." Ryan yells, once again demanding everyone's attention. "So, now can I have the ring? I want to propose properly to..."

"Uh-uh," Christy protests. "I am proposing to you."

While their family and friends laugh, they exchange rings before Ryan plasters an inappropriate-for-public kiss upon Christy's lips.

27

CONTRIBUTING TO THE DELINQUENCY OF MINORS

Maddux

"Kudos," I hiss near Brooks' ear. "This means war," I warn.

I cannot let her get the better of me. I will make it my mission to get even and one up her. How dare she ruin my plans? *The woman doesn't know who she messes with.*

"Bring it on," she counters.

She should enjoy her victory while she can.

"Dude," Ryan slaps his hand hard against my shoulder. "If you had really lost our rings..." He doesn't finish his sentence but allows the empty threat to hang there as he walks away.

We both know he can afford new rings. I'm lucky this proposal turned out to be a prank and not lost rings due to my faulty plan. It kills me that Brooks knows my nieces better than I do. She's been with them every day for five and a half years while I've barely spent a month with them. I've tried to spend as much time with them as possible, yet I can never make up for the time we lost.

I scan the crowd, finding Ryan and Christy standing among our mutual friends from the club on the opposite side of the pool. I decide to take advantage of the moment to be with my nieces. Walking towards them where they talk with Josh, I note they are still in their swimsuits.

"Hey, kiddos," I greet as I smile at Josh and Paul. "Let's go inside and change out of your suits. It's almost time for dessert." This sparks them to life.

I follow them through the patio doors then up the stairs, and I listen from the hallway as they change out of their swimsuits, excitedly talking about the desserts they plan to consume when they return.

"Uncle Maddux," the twins call for my attention.

"What may I help you with?" I ask from my new stance outside their bedroom door.

"I don't want to put on my pajamas," Harper states.

"Can we stay up past our bedtime?" Ry inquires.

"No need for pj's right now," I answer, sure I'm making the wrong parental decision. "We'll eat dessert and hide from your parents so you can stay up later."

Someone clears their throat nearby, drawing my attention to the mouth of the hall.

Brooks

I stand with my hands upon my hips, glaring at Maddux near the twins' door.

"Contributing to the delinquency of minors now I see," I tease.

I love watching the over six-foot tall man squirms with my accusation. He leans his right shoulder against the door frame, looking directly at me.

"I promised them dessert; that's all," he states.

"I distinctly recall hearing you say, '...eat dessert and hide from your parents so you can stay up later,'" I retort, smirking with one eyebrow arched.

"It's my job as uncle to allow them to get away with mischief," Maddux informs.

"If you limit them to one cupcake each, I'll help them elude their parents and bedtime," I plot.

It's his turn to raise an eyebrow at me.

"As their aunt, I, too, have a responsibility to ensure they have fun," I state.

"Touché," he chuckles.

"Ready!" the twins announce, exiting their bedroom.

28

WE HAVE A DATE

Brooks

I glance at my week's appointment schedule; I have one more appointment today, three on Wednesday the fifth, and four on Thursday the sixth. My cell phone buzzes, alerting me of an incoming text.

RYAN
free tonight?

ME
yes
if doesn't involve Maddux

RYAN
need a sitter

I only have one appointment late this afternoon.

> **ME**
> always
>
> your place or mine?

> **RYAN**
> want to celebrate setting date

> **ME**
> my place
>
> I'll pick them up in 30 mins
>
> I'll keep girls
>
> drop them off in morning

> **RYAN**
> you're the best!

> **ME**
> I won't let you forget that

> **RYAN**
> (thumbs up emoji)

I tap on my shaded appointment slot. When the information for the appointment opens, I find it's Maddux's first visit for the thigh tattoo I designed. My heart rate increases, and excitement floods me. It's a large tattoo—a unique tattoo. I love marking others with my work. I can put aside my loathing and lusting for his appointment. I will gladly endure hours creating his tattoo. I love the thought of my artwork becoming a permanent part of Maddux.

I return my purse to my lower desk drawer as the bell at the front door chimes.

"Uncle Maddux is here!" the twins scream.

Here we go. I make my way from the back towards the waiting room up front. *I can do this; I can bite my tongue while he's a customer. The twins are here. I must be polite for their sake.*

"Hi," I greet, leaning against the counter. "Let's get started."

As I walk down the hallway towards my station in my office, I sense Maddux's presence hot on my heels. He invades my safe work space. I'm no longer comfortable; I struggle to act casually. I long to snarl at him, and I fight the urge to attack.

"What are the two of you doing here?" he asks the girls as the four of us enter my area.

"Ryan texted me," I answer. "He wanted to celebrate with Christy tonight, so I volunteered to let the girls sleep over."

"That's nice of you," he responds.

"We get to watch your tattoo," the twins announce.

Maddux arches a brow in my direction. It causes me to reconsider my agreeing to let them watch. They've watched from the hallway when Christy worked here. We were careful which customers and pieces they were near. I glance at Maddux's golf shorts. Judging the leg holes, I assume he will need to remove his shorts for me to place his design. The thought of Maddux lying on my table, his shorts removed, causes my chest to tighten and my face to heat.

"Brooks," Maddux's deep voice prompts.

My eyes lift from his thighs to his blue eyes. Inappropriate thoughts about my client flood my mind as I chew on my lower lip. He extends his right hand to my left shoulder.

"Everything okay?" he inquires, eyes assessing my face.

Unable to speak, I nod.

"Where do you want me?" he asks, looking around my space.

"You'll lay here," I state as I pat my hand on the exam table. "First, I will position the transfer. You'll use that mirror to help me place it. Then, you'll lay on your stomach, and I will begin working on the back of your thigh."

He nods, excitement evident in his cerulean blue orbs.

"Change of plans, girls," I say, turning to face them. "You can play in the hallway on my iPad while I place the transfer on Uncle Maddux. When I start the needle, you can watch for a few minutes."

Disappointed, the girls nod their heads in agreement.

"Alright." Maddux claps his hands once to accentuate the word. "Head to the hall. We will call for you to come watch in a bit."

"I get the iPad first!" Harper calls as they sprint away.

"I should have worn different shorts," he thinks out loud, raising the hem of his right leg until it can no longer be raised.

I hold the transfer around his exposed thigh, but the design fits atop his shorts.

"Should I remove my shorts?" he suggests.

"If you want this design, yes," I answer. "I could make it smaller…"

"I like it as it is," he shares.

My mouth grows dry as I watch Maddux's fingers unfasten his belt, his button, then slowly lower his zipper. *I did not think this through.* A thigh tattoo seemed innocent enough until I positioned the design. I will be up close and personal with Maddux's…*boxers.*

He stands before me in snug, heather gray boxer briefs. *How will I ever be able to focus on tattooing with my hands near that large bulge in his boxers?*

Maddux clears his voice. "My eyes are up here," he smirks.

I force down the large lump in my throat, pulling my eyes from his package. With great difficulty, I position the tattoo template on his powerful thigh. Together, we reposition it. I place two small black marks upon his skin to guide me. I wet it then transfer the tracing ink onto his skins.

"I think we are ready," I announce, prompting him to lie on the table.

I stare, in awe of his muscular arms and legs as he assumes his prone position before me. Nothing can hide in his gray boxer briefs. *His butt… Dang!* He must focus on his glutes during his leg days. *This man is fine.*

"Earth to Brooks." Maddux's voice interrupts my ogling.

"Let's begin." My voice cracks, exposing my distraction. "Let me know if you need a break. I will work as fast as I can. Your adrenaline will spike, and some areas will be more sensitive than others."

"I'll be fine," he assures me.

I place the needle upon his skin, hoping my work will distract me from his firm muscles and masculine scent.

"We have a date," he says.

A date? We're not going on a date. What is he talking about?

"I don't know about you, but I thought they'd sneak off and elope rather than set a wedding date," he continues.

Ahhh. He's talking about Christy and Ryan setting a wedding date.

"They will have a beautiful wedding," I share, focused on my work.

"So, you saw it in a vision," he states. "Why do I keep forgetting you have that power?

I'm still jealous you can't see my future. When you saw their wedding, did you catch a glimpse of me?"

"When I touched Ryan that first day you came in here, I did see you standing beside him at the wedding. It's not that I can't see you. It's that I can't get visions from you. I can if you are in the visions I get from others," I explain.

"Christy mentioned you planned to talk to your guru about your inability to see my future. What did she say?" Maddux leans on his forearms, turning his head over his shoulder to look at me while I work.

"She thinks you have precognitive immunity," I share, not wanting to discuss myself. "Girls come take a peek," I call toward the hallway.

He taps on his phone screen while mumbling the words "precognitive immunity" over and over. I assume he is searching the internet for information. Knowing him, he wants a cure. He seems very interested in me predicting his future.

29

SPREADSHEETS ARE KINDA MY THING

Brooks

I pause my needle, my hand between Maddux's thighs. If I extended my fingers, I would graze... *Stop it! This is Maddux! This is the most annoying, conceited man I've met. I cannot allow myself to fantasize about him. He's Maddux!*

I force my thoughts to return to the half-finished design I've permanently placed upon his flesh. The band is complete from his outer thigh, across the back, to his inner thigh. Though his skin is angry and inflamed, the black band magnifies his strength.

"That should do it for today," I announce. "Use the mirror and let me know what you think." I place a mirror in his hand and motion to a three-way mirror against the wall.

I tidy my area while keeping my eyes on him as he turns himself at the mirror. His bulge has grown. I quickly force my eyes to my station as heat crawls up my neck and face. It seems my hands between his legs affected him as it did my thoughts.

Out of the corner of my eye, I see him adjust himself before he returns to me.

"How soon may I finish it?" he asks, standing a foot from me.

"In two to three weeks," I croak. I detest the shakiness of my voice. "Here are your care instructions." I place my hands upon his hips, urging him to spin around. "Leave this on for three hours. Then follow the after-care instructions." I place the clear, protective wrap over his newly marked skin, instruct him to redress, then motion for him to exit to the hall.

"Uncle Maddux, we're hungry," Harper announces from her coloring on the hallway floor.

"You know where the snacks are." I point to my office.

The twins look up with full on puppy-dog sad eyes and pouting lower lips. Maddux crumbles under their power.

"Let me take the three of you out to eat for dinner," he offers, looking at me. "Any place but Sonic," he adds, giving a stare to the girls when he mentions their favorite place.

"I don't think..."

"Don't think. Say yes," he encourages.

I cross my arms, my eyes scanning his face. He really wants to do this. *Why would a hot, single guy volunteer to eat dinner with two five-year-olds and me when he could open an app and hook up?* I have no doubt he is on multiple apps.

"Please! Please! Please!" Harper and Ry chant, bouncing up and down with hands in the prayer pose between us.

I roll my eyes and release a long, audible breath.

"Fine."

"Yay!" they cheer.

"You choose the restaurant." Maddux points to me.

"Uh-uh!" I shake my head. "No way. You volunteered to take us; you have to choose."

Maddux purses his lips, his eyes looking up to the right as if in thought. "Conrad's. My treat."

I nod, a slight smile forming. A flicker of warmth floods my belly.

"I need to fix an issue on the computer before we go," I state. "I spent most of the morning trying to figure it out."

"I'm good with computers," Maddux informs, motioning for me to lead the way. "Ry and Harper, please put away your coloring books and use the bathroom."

Maddux seems to be picking up on this uncle gig quickly.

"What are you working on?" he asks when I sit at my desk and open my laptop.

I point to the spreadsheet filling the screen. "I need to enter an equation for this column to find the percentage of this and this." I continue to point.

"May I?" Maddux points to the desk chair I occupy.

I stand, watching him peruse the document for a moment before he deftly types and hits enter. I stare in awe as the program works the math and displays an answer.

"How...? What...?" I stammer in disbelief.

"Spreadsheets and algorithms are kinda my thing." He shrugs, rising from my chair.

"I wish I'd known that before I wasted two hours trying to figure it out this morning," I complain.

"Think of me as your on-call I.T. guy," he chuckles. "Call me anytime you need to."

"I couldn't... You're busy..."

"You could," he argues. "It only takes me a minute."

His warm blue eyes seem earnest. *He means it.* He wants to help when I need it. The hair on the back of my neck prickles. I'm not sure how I feel about Maddux's kindness. I'm much more comfortable with our constant jabs back and forth.

He places his hand upon my arm. "Let's feed the girls before they mutiny."

30

TIME'S UP

Maddux

I stand outside the bathroom door, sipping my beer. I've only been an uncle for a month, and I am not sure of the protocol for my bathing the girls.

"Two-minute warning," Brooks announces, rising from her knees after rinsing each of the twins' hair. She stands beside me, visible to the girls in the doorway.

"Here." I pass her half-empty beer back to her.

Across the tiny bathroom, the twins splash wildly as they play in the tub. Water sloshes onto the tile wall and floor.

"I'm surprised you escaped without becoming drenched," I chuckle, scanning Brooks from head to toe.

She takes a pull from her brown beer bottle before answering, "There are rules. If they remain calm during the soap, shampoo, and conditioner, they get two minutes of free playtime before they must get out."

"And that works?" I scoff.

Her green eyes cut to mine. "So far, it does."

We watch the girls play and talk gibberish to each other. I can't get over how much they look like Ryan—and me by extension. There's no denying he is their biological father with the same eyes, hair color, curls, and height.

My time with Brooks and the twins this afternoon and evening seems easy—normal. Our feuding laid aside for a day, we've uncovered a friendship beyond our bickering barbs.

"Time's up!" Brooks' announces.

Brooks

"Good night." I flick off the lights and close the door.

I pause, listening for any movement on the other side of the door. Not hearing any, I move down the hallway.

"Think they'll fall asleep?" Maddux asks, sliding me a fresh beer.

"Here's hoping they do." I tap the neck of my beer against his.

He places his beer on the nearby counter then wraps his long fingers around my bottle, placing it by his. Our eyes lock on one another as all air seems to leave the room. A heaviness takes up residence in my stomach. I watch in stunned silence as Maddux positions his body closer, and his lips meld to mine.

My eyes remain open, peering into his. I lose myself in the blue pools as his strong, warm lips caress mine. For the first time, I allow myself to become lost in a kiss. With no visions, it's only Maddux and me in this moment.

I part my lips, opening to him, encouraging him to deepen the kiss. Maddux follows my lead. His tongue explores my mouth and tangles with mine. It's hot and heavy; it swirls my thoughts, and it consumes me. Maddux's hand at the back of my neck holds my mouth to his. I feel the kiss all the way to my toes. I long for more. I need more from him.

Too soon, he pulls his mouth from mine, gasping for breath, and places his forehead to mine. His eyes are liquid like the Caribbean. We do not speak as our chests heave rapidly. His hands upon my shoulders, his thumbs caress the bare skin of my neck.

I imagine his mouth and thumbs. A flicker of hope grows within me. For the first time, the possibility of being with a man without visions is within my reach.

"I should leave," Maddux murmurs barely above a whisper, shattering my hopes.

"Hmm?"

"Ry and Harper," he whispers.

I forgot about the twins. I allowed his kiss and touch to distract me from my duties. I lost myself in Maddux.

He skims the pad of his thumbs along my jawline from my ears toward my mouth. His forehead peels from mine, and his eyes move to my lips.

"Good night, Brooks," he growls, pulling away as if it pains him.

I watch his back all the way to my door. The sound of the latch catching jolts me from my Maddux kiss haze.

31

SUCKED OFF A CANDY CANE

Maddux

Christy, Ryan, and I coaxed Brooks into joining us for our early morning tee time on the Fourth of July. It didn't surprise me that she agreed only to ride along while we golf today.

"Let's talk colors and themes." Christy leads the conversation with Brooks as we approach our golf balls. "We need those in order to choose flowers, table settings, and everything else."

"Weeellll," Brooks chuckles, "it is your wedding, so what colors do you want?"

I take longer than I should to pull my wedge from my bag, listening in as the women speak.

"It is a summer wedding, and it is in July," Brooks thinks out loud.

At my turn, I hit too much grass behind my ball in the fairway, causing it to fall on the first cut from the green. I pour sand in my divot and quickly return to our cart.

"Gray is my favorite color," Christy reminds Brooks.

"You can't have a gray wedding," Brooks scoffs. "But you could do a dusty blue and yellow theme."

For the rest of the second hole, I try hard to focus on my golf game and not on Brooks assisting Christy with the wedding plans. Still distracted by the women on the next tee box, Ryan finally outdrives me on the par three.

"Here are some gray and dusty blue color schemes," Brooks says, showing Christy her phone as they steer past us. "Or we could choose dove—a.k.a gray—dusty blue, and yellow."

I fight my laugh as they scroll through the posts.

"You know I love my gray. I mean dove." Christy laughs. "Let's choose dove, dusty blue, and yellow."

"Yay! We made a decision," Brooks cheers, informing Ryan and me, "Shot time! We chose the color scheme for the wedding."

I like the idea of shots and promptly pour four of them into our disposable shot glasses on the seat of my golf cart.

"This is absolutely the last shot I am doing today," Christy professes. "I need to be coherent for the girls tonight. I also need to be sober to make more wedding plans," she adds, looking pointedly at her friend.

We clink our plastic glasses, downing the peppermint liquor that I packed today.

"I feel like I sucked off a candy cane," Brooks sputters.

"That can't be the worst thing you've swallowed," I retort, then promptly head toward the green, glancing over my shoulder.

Brooks opens her mouth, venom threatening to spill, but Christy halts her with her palm out.

"Please don't," she pleads. "It is only the third hole, and we have at least six more to go."

I bite back my laugh as Christy joins us on the green. After three superb tee shots, we return to the two golf carts. Brooks sits in Christy's cart, leaning against the seat back with her boot-clad feet on the dash. She's a flashing neon billboard that doesn't belong on the course in her black platform boots with too many buckles, fishnet stockings, pleated plaid skirt, and skin-tight shirt. She looks like she should work at the morgue, not ride on a golf cart at our club, and she couldn't care less what others think.

"Next decision," Brooks prompts when Christy returns to the cart. "Band or DJ?"

"DJ," the four of us say in unison and laugh.

"Open bar, right?" she asks, and we nod. "That leaves flowers."

That is my cue. I start the cart, driving towards our balls.

"Let's talk about my wedding gift," Brooks says as their cart joins ours. "I'd like to give each of you a tattoo."

"I love it!" Christy hugs her friend.

"Girls…" I feign disgust. "Not on the golf course."

Brooks opens her mouth, leaning in my direction.

"Play nice," Christy scolds. "You are upset we talked you into joining us. Don't take it out on Maddux."

Brooks scowls at me from the passenger side of the golf cart.

"I wanted to use this time to do some wedding planning with you," Christy reminds her. "We are killing two birds with one stone."

"Fine," Brooks spits.

"One of these days, I am going to talk you into golfing with me," Christy taunts.

"Good luck," Brooks scoffs.

I try to imagine Brooks in golf shoes and attire. I shake away that thought. *She's not golfing material.* Imagining her on a stripper pole? Now, that takes little imagination. *Her five-foot, eight inch body in stripper heels, bare, and gyrating against a silver pole… Damn.* I adjust my golf slacks, hoping the navy pleats in front hide my state.

32

CHEERLEADING IS NOT A SPORT

Brooks

Later, lounging by the pool in the late afternoon sun, I listen to the twins play with Ryan and Maddux in the water.

"Oh, my god," I chuckle. "Did you read this?"

Christy tilts her head.

"Read what?" she asks.

"Today's *The Back 9 Talk* post," I answer.

"Why the heck are you following that crap?" Ryan snarls, joining us at the patio table by the pool.

"I figured I needed to. Someone needs to know if they talk anymore crap about you," I defend.

"Swear jar!" Harper yells from the shallow end of the pool.

Caught up in the conversation, I did not notice the twins had moved to our end of the pool.

"Busted," taunts Maddux.

"Anyway," I drawl, giving Maddux a glare, "it sounds like we missed the drama of today's pool party at the club."

I slide my phone to Christy.

The Back 9 Talk—7/4

The Fourth of July children's pool party paused for over an hour when several children found "balloons" (a.k.a. condoms to us adults). Shame on you for ruining it for the children. Parents of prankster teenagers, rein them in at club activities and on the premises.

"Gross!" Christy cringes. "Why would someone do this to kids?"
To her horror, Ryan and Maddux chortle loudly.
"Epic," Ryan laughs.
"I wonder if they blew them up themselves or used helium?" Maddux howls.
"What's so funny?" Harper asks, climbing the pool steps.
"Nothing," Ryan and Maddux shout, causing Christy and I to giggle.
Christy does not look forward to the twins growing up, but these two already fear the dating years.
"I would opt for helium," I state.
"What?" Christy asks, unable to follow me in our conversation.
"I would never put my mouth on a…" I look sideways at the twins, who are now wrapped in towels on the nearby loungers. I shudder. "My lips do not touch prophylactics."
Ryan and Maddux chuckle like teenage boys, scrolling through the three photos included with the post.
"Grow up," I chide, plucking my phone back from them.
"Can you imagine?" Christy shakes her head in dismay.
"If my daughters found or touched those today…" Ryan growls. "Let's just say I would want someone's job."
"Let's not go there." Christy hopes to put an end to this discussion.
Ryan pulls out his phone.
"What are you doing?" she inquires.
"Hmm… Nothing," he mutters.
"Found it!" Maddux announces, extending his phone to his brother.

"Followed," Ryan states.

Seriously? These two grown men now follow the gossip blog?

Maddux

"Fuuddggee!" Ryan drawls, looking at his cell phone while he sits in a lounger at the pool's edge.

"Ummm..." the twins point in his direction. "Swear jar!"

They are making a mint with our profanities lately.

Ryan gives me a serious stare before his eyes dart to my cell phone on the table beside me. I snag my own phone, swiping to wake it.

There's a new *The Back 9 Talk* post. Judging by Ryan's reaction, this one deals with one of us.

The Back 9 Talk—7/4

A little birdie told me a new chick made an appearance on our course today. While never spotted with a club in hand, she took our club by storm.
Some members gripe that we should add an amendment to our dress code policy, limiting the surface area of skin decorated with tattoos that is visible while at the club.
These are not the only tattoo sleeves I've spotted on our tees.
While I don't judge on the basis of tattoos, I'm not sure her knee-high, punk combat boots are appropriate for golf.

Fudge is right. I'm staring at a picture shot this morning on the course. Ryan and I are in the background on the men's tee box while Christy stands beside Brooks at the golf cart. Brooks's back leans against the seatback and her booted feet are propped up on the dashboard. To those that don't know her, she looks like a punk-rock princess or a goth girl out of place on the cart.

"Brookie," Christy calls, exiting the house.

Brooks looks up from her phone. Christy searches her face for any clue she read *The Back 9 Talk* post.

"What's up, buttercup?" Brooks asks.

"Did...? There's a new..." Christy stammers.

"I saw the post," Brooks states nonchalantly.

Ryan, Christy, and I wait for her wrath. Brooks scans our faces.

"It's no big deal," she assures us. "I can't be upset; they posted the truth. I don't look like I fit in. I scare some members here, and my boots were not golf appropriate."

Christy smiles at her friend. "I love everything about you."

I study Brooks, not sure she's 100 percent cool with the post. I belong on the course, and I wouldn't be comfortable with any post about me. Brooks doesn't look like she belongs at Lynks at Tryst Falls Country Club, but the more I get to know her, the more I believe her outer armor contradicts the person inside.

Brooks

My friends doubt my sincerity about the rumor post not bothering me, but I'm used to others judging my looks. *Let them. If they judge my tattoos and attire, they won't get to know me and can't judge my personality or actions.*

I continue browsing TikTok videos as they converse around me. Occasionally, I pay attention.

"Cheerleading is not a sport," Maddux states.

"Say what?" Christy scoffs as she returns from putting the girls to bed for the night.

"You did not just claim cheerleading is not a sport," I chide, glaring at him. I mumble obscenities under my breath.

"If anything, golf is not a sport," I counter.

"Now, you are smoking crack," Maddux retorts.

"Did you just say, 'smoking crack'?" Ryan laughs at his brother.

"She's crazy to suggest golf is not a sport," Maddux defends.

"Crazy, huh?" I jibe. "Golf is a long walk where you occasionally hit a ball. Is walking a sport?"

Maddux acts personally offended by my comments.

"And you think cheerleading is a sport?"

"Do you consider gymnastics a sport?" I counter.

Ryan and Christy look back and forth between the two of us as we bicker.

"Yes," Maddux answers.

"Well," I pause, throwing my hands wide, "cheerleaders jump and tumble as they yell."

Maddux looks to his brother for help. Ryan shakes his head at him.

"Here," Ryan says, taking out his phone and thumbing to an app. "Watch this and see what you think."

I wonder what YouTube video Ryan found quickly enough to show his brother. Maddux watches the video, and I look over his shoulder. My wide eyes dart from the screen to Christy then back.

"That's Christy!" I proclaim.

Her brow furrows.

"You have a video of Christy cheering on your cell phone!" I announce in disbelief.

Maddux points to the phone screen, looking over at his brother. "You kept this video on your phone for six years?"

Ryan's sun-kissed cheeks pinken.

Maddux taps and scrolls on Ryan's phone. "Every time you bought a new cell phone, you moved these photos and videos with you."

Ryan grabs his phone back, tucking it into his shorts pocket.

"Dude," Maddux lowers his voice, stepping closer to Ryan. "I knew you loved her and missed her, but you never told me you kept these photos and videos."

I marvel at his love for Christy. *I hope someday to find a love like theirs.*

33

LET'S GET A DOG

Brooks

Three days later, a new blog post arrives as I return to Christy's pool.

The Back 9 Talk—7/7

Excrement... Foul feces... Nasty #2... Fragrant fecal... Dirty doo-doo... Smelly sh!t... Pungent poop... Big BM... Dark dung... Massive manure... Wicked waste... Stinky stool...
Do you pick up your pet's piles of poo?
The club is cracking down on members that walk their dogs on the trails, cart paths, or other areas of the course and do not bag their bowel movements. This is your warning; they plan to run DNA testing to determine the breeds of the frequent offenders. Use the walking trails with bags and receptacles or stay in your own yard.
Sh!t happens, but not on our golf course.

"Daddy!" the twins greet.

"Can I get in?" Ryan asks, rounding the shallow end of the pool. "Ladies, you look like you are having fun," he teases, pointing to the slushy red concoction in the pitcher before us.

"Mr. Josh made us strawberry daiquiris." Christy grins.

"It is hard work, watching the girls swim in the sweltering heat," I explain.

Ryan's eyes return to Christy.

"I think we should get a dog," he declares.

"Seriously?" Christy sputters.

"I guess you read the recent rumor post," I laugh.

"As if our lives aren't crazy enough with the girls, you want to bring a puppy into it?" Christy continues her disbelief.

"What kind of dog are you thinking about?" I question.

Ryan shrugs, tapping on his cell phone screen then raising it to his ear.

"Who are you calling?" Christy asks.

"Hey, Maddux," Ryan greets, shooting a wink at us. "I am thinking about getting a dog."

My face pinches at Maddux's name, and Christy acts put off that Ryan called him.

"We are in the pool," Ryan informs him before disconnecting the call.

"Why did you call him?" I spit.

Sometimes, I believe Ryan loves fueling the flames of dislike Maddux and I share any time he gets the chance.

"It looked like the two of you did not like my suggestion that we get a puppy, so I called for reinforcements," Ryan confesses, standing at the edge of the pool. "Cannon ball!" he yells, jumping into the air as he wraps his arms around his knees.

He sinks to the bottom of the shallow end of the pool, ensuring he splashes everyone. He surfaces, a proud smile upon his face, to hear the cheers of his daughters and the stifled curses of us ladies on the pool deck.

"Throw me, Daddy," Harper encourages.

He takes turns lifting the girls, his hands at their waists, and throwing them towards the diving board end of the pool. They squeal as they flail their arms in the air before plunging into the deep end and cheering when they resurface.

"What's all this noise?" Maddux yells over the railing of the deck above us.

"Uncle Maddux!" the twins greet.

"Yay… Maddux is here," I say sarcastically to Christy's right.

"Be nice," she warns, filling her glass again.

"I like spending time with my best friend and wish that, sometimes, it was just us," I grumble. "It is like Ryan can't stand to be outnumbered."

"Now, about this dog…" Maddux raises his voice loudly enough for us to hear. "I think it is a terrific idea." He looks at me. "Pets teach responsibility and love. A dog or two would be good for all of you."

"Oh, no. We are not getting two puppies," Christy responds firmly.

"Good. Then we agree on one," Ryan states, a sly grin upon his face.

"Now, what size and breed?" Maddux prompts, furthering the discussion.

"It is none of your business," I bite in his direction.

"My brother called me to discuss getting a dog. That makes it my business," he counters.

"Let's table the puppy conversation until the girls go to bed," Christy suggests. "Until then, the four of us can think on it."

34

A MILLION THINGS

Brooks

Monday, the bell above the door tinkles as a customer enters. I am pleased to find it's someone I know.

"Ryan," I greet, surprised.

"Brooks, I am in desperate need of your help," he states.

My face pinches. "What's wrong?"

"Oh, sorry," he assures me. "Nothing is wrong. I have…" He digs into his shorts pocket for his excuse for coming here today. "I came for a tattoo if you have an opening. I know you are busy, so I could…"

"My two o'clock canceled," I inform him. "So, you are in luck. Let's see the drawing."

I extend my hand toward him.

Before he slips his design my way, he confesses, "And I need some advice while I am here."

That is the real reason for his showing up unannounced at my parlor. I take the folded paper in hand.

He explains, "The twins designed it, and I want to surprise them by really getting the tattoo."

I nod. "They love drawing tattoos."

He smiles proudly, and he watches as I place the girls' drawing on my scanner.

"Where are we placing this one?" I ask.

"I want it visible to me and others," he tells me.

"We could do your bicep." I study the design again. "I could shrink it small enough for your neck or your wrist."

"Yes!" He turns over his arm, displaying his inner wrist. "If you can make it fit, I want it here."

I smile. "Give me a sec."

I fiddle with my laptop while he looks at the designs framed on my walls.

"Follow me," I direct, already walking down the hall.

I apply black gloves over my blue ones and prompt him to sit.

"I am surprised the twins didn't insist on coming with you today."

"They don't know I am doing this," he admits.

My smile grows wider. "They are going to freak out."

"I know," he agrees.

"You must film it for me," I declare. "Please promise me you will ask Christy to film it when you show them."

"Or you could be there when I show them?" he suggests.

I look up and to the left for a moment before I answer. "I have no other appointments, but I can't unexpectedly close the shop."

"You are the owner," he reminds me.

"I get relieved at four. I could text to see if he can come in at 3:30." I think out loud. "Position this where you want it."

I lay the tattoo template on the table by his wrist before grabbing my phone to text. Turning back, I adjust his tattoo placement a bit.

"Ready?" I ask.

"Bring it," he taunts.

I waste no time in starting my needle and inking his flesh.

"While I work, you should tell me the real reason you dropped in today," I prompt, glancing up at him briefly.

"I wouldn't mind if you removed your gloves. You could answer all my questions and then some," Ryan chuckles, only half teasing.

"If I could pick and choose what I see, I would be more apt to oblige," I say, still focused on my work. "There is no promise I would find what you're hoping for, and trust me, there are some things between Christy and you that I should never see."

I dab a bit of blood and ink from his wrist.

"What's got you…um… What do you want to talk about?"

Ryan sighs deeply. "A million things," he mumbles.

"Like what?"

"Like…" He decides to let it all out. "Do I make Christy happy? Are the three of them better with me in their lives? Should the girls attend public or private school? Should we get a nanny? Is Christy taking another job a good fit for our family? Are we a family? I mean, we live under one roof, but are we becoming a family? Should I push for the three of them to attend my away games?"

"Is that all?" I interrupt, laughing and sitting back on my rolling stool, crossing my arms over my chest.

Ryan looks down at his wrist to find his tattoo finished. Although the irritated skin is red, it's perfect. He smiles at me, nervous to hear my words of wisdom.

I cover his tattoo as I speak. "You are a new father. Most of your concerns are normal for any parent. You will doubt yourself and worry until the day you die. Christy has more practice at it, but she still toils over every decision. Ryan, the girls love you. Christy loves you. And…" I pause, pursing my lips in thought. "Christy will kick my butt if you tell her what I am about to tell you."

I wait for his approval; Ryan nods.

"That day that Maddux and you first walked into my tattoo parlor and I shook your hand, I saw things."

"Christy asked me long ago not to give her any hints when I see visions, so I don't. Well, I did hint by saying, 'Happily ever after.'" I shrug. "After touching your hand, I went home and touched both girls to see their futures. I wanted confirmation. I saw a blindside in my best friend's future, and I needed to see from another source. I saw you."

"You've got to tell me," Ryan pleads. "I won't tell Christy. I need something, anything to help me."

"Ryan, you are all four right where you are meant to be. I saw the four of you happy and healthy for many years to come. It killed me not to tell Christy that night that she would bump into you and that the four of you would make a beautiful family."

I start cleaning up the area.

"I had to let you scare the crap out of her. I had to let Ry break her arm, and I had to let the two of you talk it out."

"But you saw other stuff further in the future?" he pries.

I grin. "Ryan, I try to avoid having visions and am not practiced at sharing them with people I am close to."

"Ah… I am growing on you," he teases.

"Actually, the visions make it easy to let you in. I mean, since you will be sticking around and are good for my bestie." I rise, crossing my arms over my abdomen, and continue, "All I will tell you is that I see your family many years from now, happy and healthy. I even saw your daughters and sons watching you play for the Cardinals well into the future."

My eyes grow wide, and my hand flies to my mouth, suddenly aware I divulged more than I planned to.

"Sonnnsss?" Tears well in Ryan's eyes.

"Ryan," I point at him. "You can't ever, and I mean ever, tell Christy. She is going to kill me for talking to you. I knew I shouldn't start telling you anything. Once my mouth starts, it is hard for me to filter myself. Ryan… Are you hearing me?"

He nods, unable to articulate more than that.

"She can never even get a *hint* that I told you about that—any of that." I am still pointing at him.

He raises his right hand. "I promise."

"And you need to wipe that smile off your face. Your knowing grin will get us both into trouble," I demand.

"I will hide it by the time I get home," he vows.

Ryan bends down, placing a peck on my cheek, causing a vision from his upcoming wedding to play through my mind.

"Don't touch me," I mumble.

"Wanna ride with me? I will surprise the fam with ice cream when we bring you home."

I shoo him out of the room, waving my hand.

"Give me five minutes."

35

A MONTH'S WORTH OF VISIONS

Brooks

All cleaned up and ready to surprise the twins, I pass my closer, Miguel, in the hallway. I make to speak to him, but he is a man on a mission. I swipe my thumb across my phone screen, waking it up. My mind on my phone, I cannot react when my feet slip out from under me.

My feet fly up as my body falls down. I stare in horror as Ryan attempts to break my fall, to protect my head, but he can't get across the room in time. He watches as the back of my head bounces on the polished concrete floor. Panic floods my veins.

"Damn!" Miguel shouts, emerging from the back room.

"Get towels," Ryan orders, pointing for him to turn around.

"Lie still," Ryan instructs me.

As Ryan's hands hold my shoulders in place, the visions begin. I need to tell him not to touch me, but I can't form the words while the visions hit me like a tsunami.

Tee ball, football, swimming, pool parties…

He scans my scalp, gently moving his fingertips to the back of my head. His fingers pause at the same time I hiss. Pulling his hand away, his fingers are red. He places his palm over the cut despite my groans.

I attempt to get up; he keeps me on the floor with his free arm.

Family Christmases, birth of babies, the four of us golfing...

"Easy. You could have a neck or spine injury," he warns.

"I'm fine," I spit, finally able to form words. "I can wiggle my toes and my fingers. Stop touching me!"

Miguel returns with two white hand towels. Ryan immediately replaces his hand with a towel; I take advantage of his movement to ignore his concern and sit up. I squeeze my eyes shut tight.

Wine tastings, the Espys, investments...

"I'm fine," I state, unable to stop the visions from playing rapidly in my brain.

Ryan shakes his head. "You're bleeding," he argues. "You need stitches."

"No, I don't," I bite.

Ryan places the palm of his hand over my wound, showing me the blood-soaked towel.

"Head wounds bleed a lot..." I spout. Then, my eyes roll backwards, and the world goes dark.

"She's coming to," the stranger's voice says from above me.

My vision is blurry as I watch Ryan tossing a saturated towel into the biohazard waste can.

Visions flood my mind, but Ryan's no longer touching me.

"Can you hold this to her scalp for me? I need another set of hands."

Blinking, I notice blue scrubs in front of me.

Ryan bends at my bedside, holding the gauze to the back of my head. Almost instantly, the room grows dark again.

When the staff wheels me back into the exam room, I find Ryan and Christy waiting anxiously for me.

Sweet 16 party for the twins, their first dates...

"Well?" Ryan prompts the staff for my diagnosis.

"I have a concussion and a sprained wrist," I inform my friends.

The medical staff releases me into the care of my two friends with instructions and concussion protocols to follow.

Engagement rings, the Super Bowl, another Super Bowl...

Christy sits in the back seat of her car with me, and Ryan drives.

"What the hell?" I grumble when we round the corner near my apartment.

"You will need to park on the other side of the square," Christy directs. "I can't believe it is this full."

Ryan insists on carrying me to the tattoo shop, we spot an off-duty police officer directing traffic on the sidewalk. A line forms at the door to the parlor and extends down the block.

Visions of Ryan assault me. *Why won't they stop?*

Not liking the crowd, Ryan instructs, "Christy, hurry to the door. I will carry Brooks upstairs, then I will see what is going on down here."

In my periphery, I see cell phones aimed in our direction as Ryan carries me past Christy, ascending the stairs. He places me safely on my sofa.

"No more touching! Can I have my cell phone?" I demand immediately.

"No screen time," Christy reminds me.

"Then I need you to call Madam Alomar," I growl. "Do it now. Tell her to come here. It's urgent."

"Did you say 'Madame Alomar'?" Ryan asks in disbelief.

"Out! Now!" I bark, pointing him to the door.

Not wanting to upset me further, he heads toward the door.

"Call me if you need me," he tells Christy. "I will be downstairs."

He kisses Christy before leaving.

"For the love of god, do not let Ryan back in my apartment," I order.

"He's only trying to help," Christy assures.

"He's causing visions without touching me," I inform. "Just being in the same room with him starts them, and it's killing my head."

Christy's eyes widen. She mouths, "Without touching?"

I nod. "That hurts," I moan, my hands flying to the sides of my head.

"Stop moving," she chides in her mom voice. "Lay still."

"Call Madam Alomar," I groan.

"I am!" she scolds. "Calm your jets."

I've experienced a month's worth of visions in a couple of hours. *Calm my jets... I've seen... I've seen... Maddux was in most of the visions, and so was I...*

36

ALL IN

Maddux

I run my palm against the stubble of my jaw, pretending to ponder my bid as I scan the table counterclockwise once more. To my right, the pompous douchebag holds an ace with a two. Beside him, the downtown skyrise mogul holds a five and a ten, and to my left, the multiple trust fund, old-money heir holds a king and a jack.

I feel my phone vibrate in the breast pocket of my jacket. *Not now. I'm about to win.*

I push a stack of poker chips to the center. *Forty thousand dollars should raise their hackles.* All eyes widen before darting to my face. *Yes. I just did that. Fold now or regret it.*

My cell vibrates yet again. I ignore it. *I'm working.* The guy to my right folds. *Smart man.* Next guy pushes 40 thousand toward the middle. To his right, the trust fund baby ponders for long moments before reluctantly pushing his final 40 thousand to the center of the green felt. In his eyes, I recognize fear; too late, he figures out I chose to up by 40 thousand because it is all he had left.

Gotcha!

I turn over my cards.

"Damn!" the guy to my left groans.

The dealer slowly slides my plethora of chips towards me. Internally, I gloat; externally, I exude confidence and restraint.

Now, who could that be? My cell vibrates, alerting an incoming call in my pocket. I ignore it, remaining focused on the poker table before me.

Before I turn over my newly dealt cards, I raise the bid 50 thousand. My two remaining opponents stare wide-eyed in my direction.

"Perhaps the final hand, gentlemen?" our dealer announces to the table.

Yep. You're going down clowns.

I'm done nursing them along.

They go through the motions until it's my turn again. I purposefully raise one thousand, knowing the two remaining players are out of funds. They both fold, leaving me with a three and a nine for the win.

I glance at my Rolex to find we've played for only two and a half hours tonight. I make a mental note to draw it out next month and to lose more before I win. *Perhaps I should tell the crew I will play the loser;* it's a role I rarely volunteer for. I can't let the others become suspicious. For once, I'll lose and play the humble role for a night.

"Gentlemen, it's been a pleasure," I brag, rising as I motion for a nearby server to cash in my chips for me. I spend at least ten minutes conversing with the losers from my table and others that hang around to witness multiple poker table wins while I await my money.

As soon as the green cash is handed to me in a secure black duffle, I say my goodbyes and exit. Normally, I hang around, watching everything play out. Tonight, I have texts and phone calls waiting for me.

Once through the door, I look at my cell phone.

Crap!

37

ALL HANDS ON DECK

Maddux

"Yo!" I interrupt the conversation around the kitchen island. "What's so important that you blew my phone up tonight?"

Seeing my brother, Christy, Josh, and Paul casually talking around the kitchen like life is perfect, I cannot imagine any reason for Ryan to call me five times and text me over ten times tonight. I look from Ryan to Christy and back, waiting for this big news that seemed so urgent only hours ago.

"You didn't text him to tell him everything was okay?" Christy swats Ryan's shoulder. "Maddux, I'm sorry," she assures. "He never should have left you hanging all night."

I fight my laughter at her scolding Ryan.

"Dude, where were you?" Ryan asks, looking me up and down.

It doesn't escape me that I am not normally dressed in my designer suit, dress shirt, and cuff links at ten on a Monday night. Most days, I am in golf attire or my swimsuit by dinner.

"I had a work thing," I state. *It's not a total lie.* There are aspects to my work that my brother and friends are not aware of.

"A work date?" Christy inquires, smirking hopefully.

"Nah. Just business," I promise. "Now, what is up with all of the texts and calls?"

"Miss Brooks fell," Josh informs, taking pity upon me.

"Is she—"

Christy interrupts my concern. "Brooks is fine. She has a concussion and sprained wrist; she needs rest, but she is fine."

"How?" I sputter.

"The dumb kid that works for her spilled coffee," Ryan further explains. "Before he could mop it up, Brooks fell."

"Ryan took her to the ER for stitches and scans," Christy continues. "She'll be fine, but she's experiencing…"

"Visions," Ryan finishes for Christy.

"That's not new," I scoff.

"She's having visions about me without me touching her," Ryan brags. "I only need to enter the room, and she has visions."

I tilt my head and squint my eyes at my brother. *I'm… I'm…jealous. She cannot get a vision from my touch, but now she can have visions without touching Ryan…? It is unfair. What's so special about my little brother?*

"Something happened when I placed my hand on her bleeding head wound," Ryan answers unspoken question. "Madam Alomar says my hand in her blood formed a connection. She hopes to help Brooks control this new connection. So, she may block me out."

"Hold on," I interrupt, holding out my palm towards my brother. "Did you say, 'Madam Alomar'?" I cannot stifle my laughter.

"That's what they call her," Ryan defends.

"So, Brooks is okay? And the parlor is okay?" I seek confirmation.

Christy nods. "She's a little battered at the moment, but she is still the same outspoken, iron-willed Brooks."

"It was all hands on deck," Josh shares. "While Ryan and Christy were at the hospital with Miss Brooks, we…" He motions his finger between Paul and himself. "We helped the twins answer the phones and schedule appointments."

My brow furrows. "The twins?"

"Yes," Josh affirms. "When they heard Ryan's message about Miss Brooks at the ER, they couldn't wait at home for word. They wanted to go to the tattoo parlor, and once there—when things stormed out of control—we helped."

"Once Ryan's social media post went live, fans wanted tattoos," Paul shares. "It was all hands on deck."

"So, while I went to a boring work event tonight, Ryan rescued Brooks, tweeted about it, and her business exploded...? Sounds like I missed quite a night," I nearly growl.

Brooks convolutes every part of my life. I think of her constantly. One minute, she infuriates me, and the next, I want her. I want her in a way I've never yearned for any other woman. And now, she is hurt. She's at home, alone, hurting, and I cannot go to her tonight. It wouldn't look right if I let her know this late that I am worried about her.

38

I MET YOUR MOM

Maddux

"She should not be accepting visitors," An old crone grouches. "Put da bags dere. I'm on my way out."

Weird. I stand, unsure what to do now that I placed the takeout food on the counter. After she exits, I scan the space, looking for Brooks.

I hear the faint sound of the toilet flushing and water running before she emerges from the hall.

"Oh!" She startles at my presence in the kitchen. "What are you doing here?"

"I brought your favorite Chinese," I state as my excuse for dropping by. "Your mom seems nice."

"What?" Brooks chortles, immediately holding the sides of her head. "Don't make me laugh; it hurts."

"I'm sorry." I point to the door. "I met your mom."

"She is not my mom," Brooks states.

"Oh, I'm sorry." I back pedal. "I assumed…"

"Madam Alomar is my mentor," Brooks explains. "She's helping me… Um… She's trying to teach me to…"

"Ryan told me about your new visions," I offer as a rescue from her rambling explanation. "Did she help you?"

Brooks shrugs. "We will see. Shall we eat?"

I motion for her to choose a stool as I remove the cardboard containers from the bags. She mentioned on the night I hung out with her and the twins after my first tattoo that Chinese from the Liberty Hy-Vee grocery store was her favorite. Although she doesn't admit it, I know she is surprised I remembered.

"What are you doing here?" Brooks demands between bites of General Tso's chicken.

"I had an appointment," I quip.

She flinches. "I'll need to set you up to finish your tattoo with someone else," she offers, thinking I'm serious.

"I want you to finish it," I inform.

"Have to heal my wrist," she waves her splinted right wrist between us.

"I thought someone with your level of talent would be ambidextrous," I tease.

"Did Christy send you?" she asks, scooping a second helping onto her plate.

"No. Why?"

"I'm trying to figure out your angle," she answers honestly.

"No angle," I return. "You are hurt, and I..."

I...I what? I didn't sleep at all last night, worrying about her. It should have been me with her in the ER; it should have been me lifting her into my arms and whisking her away. I long to stop pretending.

Brooks

And I...what? Why is he here? I am not in the mood to spar. Mental quips... I just can't today.

What is Maddux doing here…in my apartment?
Did he take the day off?

He isn't in his designer suit for work. He isn't in a polo and golf slacks for the club. He's in a royal blue, snug ,V-neck T-shirt, shorts, and blue Sperry boat shoes.

This is casual Maddux…in my apartment. What the hell is going on?

"It was too late to check on you last night when I learned the news of your fall," Maddux informs. "I figured you still needed to eat, so I brought you lunch." His smile doesn't portray his usual confidence.

"Well, thank you for this," I motion my fork to the three containers of Chinese food. "I didn't know I was even hungry until I smelled it."

"Even with a concussion, you need to eat," he chuckles. His chuckle morphs into a laugh he cannot suppress.

"What's so funny?" I challenge.

"The twins have pajamas like those," he confesses.

I glance down at my *Nightmare Before Christmas* sleep set. "I bought the four of us matching pj's for Christmas last year."

My statement causes him to laugh louder. I raise an eyebrow in challenge.

"So, Christy has a pair, too?" he asks between chuckles.

I nod.

"They're cute."

He thinks my pajamas are cute. This little tidbit thrills me.

"Shall we watch a movie?" Maddux offers. "Or maybe two this afternoon?"

Clearly, Ryan and Christy did not give him the concussion protocol regarding screen time. I should decline, but a big part of me wants to watch two movies with him this afternoon. It's not so much the movies; it's spending hours with him. I can't focus enough to read right now, and computer screens bother my eyes. *Lounging on the sofa with Maddux sounds like the perfect way to pass the time.*

39

YOU SHOULD WRITE GREETING CARDS

Maddux

"Knock, knock," I call from a tiny crack in the doorframe. "I'm looking for the Maid of Honor."

"Come in," Christy invites, signaling they are decent.

"Special delivery," I announce, unable to say more as my throat grows dry.

Christy looks beautiful in her white robe with her hair and makeup complete. However, it is Brooks standing on the far side of the room in her dove gray, sexy, floor-length dress that calls to me. The spaghetti straps, with the slip-like fabric drapes over her body, leaving very little to the imagination; there's no way she wears underwear or a bra for that matter. She stands with her right leg outstretched, drawing my eyes to the slit, which reveals her long, toned legs and provides a peek at her red and black bouquet of roses—a tattoo on her thigh.

"Uncle Maddux is being funny," Harper giggles, walking past me to join Brooks and her mother.

"I'm dropping off two girls," I state. "But I need to hurry back."

"What's wrong?" Christy panics.

I raise my palms between us. "Nothing is wrong. I promised I would hurry. That is all."

"Ryan is okay? Is he nervous?" she asks, her hands clasped in her lap at the make-shift vanity.

"Nervous, yes," I chuckle. "He's ready for the afterparty and honeymoon."

"He will be ready for photos in 20 minutes," Brooks states instead of asking after looking at the time on her nearby cell phone.

"I'll take care of my best man duties. You worry about yours." I look around the attic space. "Ry and Harper, Miss Brooks is now in charge of you." With that announcement, I close the door behind me, protecting myself from the gorgeous woman, save for the stunning picture in my mind.

"Ready?" I ask from the doorway, striking a pose, leaning against the door frame in my cream and dusty blue Cuban shirt and khaki slacks. I am glad Christy opted for a casual summer wedding instead of tuxes. Today's high is 90 degrees; *a tux would be miserable.*

"You're ready," I answer for my brother. "You have been ready since the day she popped back into your life."

"I'm ready," Ryan agrees. "But I'm more ready for the ceremony to be over. I'm ready for our happily ever after."

"You're just nervous about your vows," I surmise, and he nods.

"Public speaking doesn't bother me, but not cracking jokes while doing so does," he admits.

"They're your vows. If you want to joke, you should," I state.

"I can't use humor and make light of our love," he argues.

I place my hands upon his shoulders, all traces of my smile gone. "Christy asked you to write your vows. She loves you and expects the real you to speak. The Ryan that she loves is honest and fun-loving. That is the guy she wants standing with her at the altar today."

Ryan pulls a note card from his pants pocket, tearing it to shreds over a trash can.

"Let's do this," he announces, following me from the room.

As we emerge from the employee break room at the back of the kitchen, we are greeted by the kitchen and wait staff. Slowly, we ease our way through the busy workers into the dining space where Ryan is caught off guard by the family members and guests that have arrived early.

"I forgot about the cocktail hour," he murmurs near my ear.

I chuckle, patting his shoulder. "As your best man, I'm supposed to help you socialize with guests when we're not posing for wedding photos," I inform.

"Dude," I chuckle. "Breathe. You are turning green."

Ryan closes his mouth, drawing long breaths in and out through his nose. I keep my eyes trained on his.

"I forgot everything," my brother confesses.

"Your vows?" I quirk a brow.

"No. Everything." He waves his hands around the space we stand in. "The pregame, kickoff time, everything."

I chortle and nervously scan the area, afraid others will hear us.

"This is not a football game," I remind him through my laughter. "You said pregame and kickoff. We are at your wedding."

I shake my head, moving beside him as I rest my arm across his shoulders.

"I've got you," I promise. "I'll take you where you need to be and tell you what to do. Right now, we are to greet your guests while we wait for the photographer to find us."

Ryan nods, looking around the large room, unsure who to approach first. Fortunately for him, our parents join us.

"He looks a little green around the gills," Dad tells me.

"Honey…" Mom takes Ryan's hand in hers. "I peeked into the attic. Christy looks lovely. She will be down any minute to start the photos."

"Chin up," Dad orders. "It is not the defensive line of the Grizzlies; she is to be your wife."

"I can't let Christy see my nerves. I don't want her to confuse them for doubt of my love for her. Talk to me," Ryan begs of me, and I nod.

"T-minus one hour," he jests before I can speak up. "I'm ready to wear a ring and move on to the afterparty."

Our father chuckles, and our mother shakes her head.

"What?" Ryan defends. "I am being honest. I'm sure Christy would say the same."

As we carry on a conversation with our family, the photographers snap photos from every angle.

"Right about now, I am wishing I had paid closer attention to Christy when she shared the details about the wedding she planned," Ryan admits.

"There are five photographers," I explain. "Three will be taking candid shots while two will be posing the wedding party around the vineyard."

Ryan's smile conveys how happy he is that I listened to Christy's details. I have his back today.

"It really is hard not to make eye contact with them as they snap pictures," Mom states, her eyes motioning in the direction of the photographers. "I hope Christy's boss, Ty, recognizes how big of a favor you are doing for him by letting them use photos from your wedding."

"Didn't Dad tell you?" I answer for him. "Ryan and I invested in Ty's vineyard. So, Ryan and Christy's wedding is serving as a launching point for our joint business."

"You own a vineyard?" Mom both asks and exclaims. "I hope that means I get to taste copious amounts of wine."

"Sorry to interrupt, but the photographer is signaling they are ready for us," I state, waving across the room.

"*Ciao*," Mom calls as we walk away.

Ryan chuckles. "Her Italian lessons are paying off."

I laugh with him, "Dare you to tell her it is '*Arrivederci.*'"

He shakes his head, holding the door for me. Ryan freezes in his tracks after rounding the side of the building, taking in the scene Christy created for the vow ceremony.

In the shade of a ginormous white, open-sided tent, white cloth-covered chairs are lined up at angles toward the center aisle. At center stage stands a large bamboo trellis, draped with a thin dusty blue and gray fabric with yellow flowers. The beautiful display before the field of vines moves the groom.

"I need a favor," Ryan tells me. "I want to buy the trellis for my yard."

I bump my shoulder with his. "My brother, the romantic," I tease.

"Just do it for me," he orders. "No matter what it costs. I want that exact one, not one like it."

I nod, now understanding he's serious.

"Gentlemen," the photographer's assistant calls to us, "we are ready for the best man right here and the groom here."

For ten minutes, I pose with Ryan and then our parents within the romantic scene Christy created before I lead him back to the cocktail hour. I hover nearby as Ryan nibbles on shrimp and as he moves amongst the crowd. His nerves evaporate as he speaks with his teammates and neighbors. That is until I tell him it's time for more photos.

"Are you ready to see your bride?" I murmur.

Instantly, the hair on the back of my neck rises, and my heartbeat quickens. I'm about to see her again. Christy and Brooks will be posing with us now before the couple exchanges their vows. While they are both superstitious, Ryan and Christy felt not seeing each other before the ceremony was unnecessary.

Ryan is standing at the altar, like he would be if they had waited, when he sees her for the first time. In a wispy, ivory sundress, she walks up the aisle towards him, smiling widely.

My heartbeat pounds in my ears, and my body sparks to life at the sight of Christy's Maid of Honor. My fingers tingle with the need to caress her bare, sun-kissed shoulders, which the spaghetti straps display, and I lick my lips, longing to kiss her. I should not have this reaction to Christy's friend. I need to be focused on my brother and my duties on his special day.

"Hello, Mr. Harper," Christy greets, assuming the position beside my brother for the photographer.

"Hello, soon-to-be Mrs. Harper," he returns with a smile.

It's not lost on me that Brooks wipes the inside corner of her eyes, and my mother frantically searches for a tissue at the sight of the happy couple. I attempt to focus on Ryan and the photographers while sneaking glances at Brooks in her long, elegant gown.

Time passes in a blur. Before I know it, it's Ryan's turn to share his vows.

"When you proposed writing our own vows, I knew it would be a monumental task to put into words all you mean to me. I do not like to fail, so here it goes. You are a hole in one..."

As the crowd interrupts his vows with raucous laughter, he is forced to pause. He spent over a week perfectly picking his words, and he chose to throw them away two hours ago.

"Bear with me," he begs the guests. "I am a simple man, and while I'm up here in front of my closest friends and family, I ask that you not judge me as I spill my heart to this magnificent woman."

While *ahh*s sweep through the crowd, he takes a deep breath to steady his nerves and collect his thoughts before he continues. I watch as he spins the engagement ring on her finger.

"Christy, you are an expertly grilled steak and a Super Bowl victory rolled into one." My brother ignores chuckles as he continues. "From the day you chose the seat beside me in my senior calculus class, I have been under your spell. Though we spent time apart, my heart always belonged to you, and it always will. I can't wait to spend the next 80 years in love with my sexy-as-hell wife."

He kisses the back of Christy's hand as a blush creeps upon her cheeks, and the tent erupts with catcalls and applause.

"You should write greeting cards when you retire," I say over his shoulder.

40

2 FINGERS, 1 WORD

Brooks

"Ladies," Maddux greets, walking toward us.

"Do not look now, but the uptight suit is approaching," I grumble, hot and ready to shed this long dress.

"Be nice; you're in public," he chides. "I'm here to remind you the twins need to leave in about an hour. So—"

I interrupt, "We need to cut the cake, dance the first dance, and throw the bouquet." I begin scanning the area for Ryan.

"Ry, Harper, and Ryan are making their way to the cake as we speak," he informs, his smirk aimed at me.

"May I escort the two of you?" Maddux offers his arms to us.

Christy slips her arm through his elbow; I hesitate before begrudgingly following her lead. Arm in arm, the three of us make our way toward the twins, who are waving from in front of the wedding cake. I note the photographers flanking them from every direction, snapping numerous photos.

"Who is ready to eat some cake?" I ask the girls, causing excited squeals.

"Shall we?" Ryan asks, entwining his arm with Christy's.

The couple assumes their spot behind the three-tiered cake, Ry between Christy and me while Harper stands between Ryan and Maddux. The DJ cuts the music, and all eyes swing in our direction. With a raised voice, Maddux announces it's time to cut the cake.

"Do it, Daddy!" Harper cheers.

"Behave," Christy warns, not wanting icing smeared all over her face.

Ryan's crooked grin does nothing to ease her worries. It's the same smile I've seen on Maddux. On their own, my eyes flicker to him. I lose myself in the shape of his lips and the glimmer in his eyes. It causes a flutter in my belly and excites every part of me.

Focus. Focus. Focus. There are hours left here before I can escape.

Christy carefully feeds Ryan a piece of cake, ready to pose for a few photos and move on to the next item on the itinerary.

"My turn!" Harper announces. "Do me! Do me!"

Ryan and Christy exchange glances. He nods then cuts two small pieces of cake. He hands her a slice and takes one in his hand.

"Ready?"

She nods. At the same time, they squat. She feeds Ry while he feeds Harper. The girls giggle as cameras flash from every angle.

"Time to toss the bouquet," Maddux instructs, taking his best man duties seriously. "Brooks, gather the single ladies, and I will make the announcement."

I watch as he walks to the DJ stand, taking the microphone in hand.

"May I have your attention please?" Maddux's voice sounds smooth and sultry over the sound system. "In a moment, Mrs. Harper will toss her bouquet, so all the single women should make their way to the left side of the dance floor. Now, it is time for the couple's first dance. This will not be the traditional first dance between Mr. and Mrs. Harper. The couple opted to share this dance as a family. Ry, Harper, Christy, and Ryan, please make your way to the center of the dance floor." He returns the mic to the DJ and moves to watch beside me.

Christy bends between the girls. "You know that TikTok dance you like to practice?"

They nod.

"Think you can do it with Daddy and me right now?"

Again, they nod.

"But who is going to record?" Harper asks.

Christy points where I stand with a cell phone aimed at the four of them. Both girls wave excitedly, and I wave back.

Ryan signals the DJ, and the four of them strike the first pose. When the music starts, they perform the dance routine as the guests laugh and cheer them on. The girls jump up and down excitedly when the song ends.

"We did it! We did it!" the twins cheer. "Miss Brooks, did you record us?"

I nod, extending my phone for the girls to see the video. Josh instructs me to share it with him so he can post it on Christy's social media for Ryan's female fans to see.

"Time to throw the bouquet," the DJ announces.

We hurry to complete the traditional tasks before the twins make their exit.

I take the girls by their hands, walking them toward the other women. Maddux hands Christy her bouquet. Ryan spins her away from the guests and plants a chaste kiss on her lips before retreating to the edge of the dance floor.

She holds her left hand in the air, extending fingers as she counts. "One...two...three!"

She places both hands on the stems and launches the bouquet over her head, behind her back. She immediately spins as the flowers hit me in the shoulder and fall into my reluctant hands. I quickly toss it to the twins to my right and wipe my hands on my dress. I act like it was coated in cooties before being launched towards me.

The DJ restarts the music, and the guests return to their seats or take to the dance floor. Christy joins me and the girls as Ryan and Maddux approach.

"Congrats on catching the bridal bouquet," Maddux says to me. "I think that means you are the next to get married."

"Two words, one finger." I spit venom back at him.

"Touchy," Maddux continues to prod.

"Truce," Christy demands, looking between us. "Harper and Ry, you have 15 minutes to dance before you go home."

In a flash, the two find a spot in front of the DJ to bust a move. Ryan and Christy disperse into the crowd to mingle with their guests. I remain at her side and Maddux with Ryan.

After half an hour, I tap Christy on the shoulder. "Sorry to interrupt, but you need to see this," I say under my breath, bending between Gibson and Christy as they sit for a bit. "Ryan's friends are shedding shirts. We. Are. The. Luckiest women alive."

They follow my gaze across the barn to see the Cardinals quarterback, wide receiver, running back, and kicker dancing—sans shirts—for a group of laughing women.

"I am going in," Ryan announces from behind us.

We watch in stunned silence as he jogs toward his teammates while unbuttoning the front of his shirt. Like a stripper, he teases with his shirt before tossing it into the crowd of nearby tables where it lands on, of all people, his mother. He joins the others in moves that remind me of *Magic Mike*.

"No way..." I interject.

Following my line of sight, the others find Maddux on the far-left side of the barn, removing his shirt. Christy looks back to me, finding I'm unable to pull my eyes from him. I watch as the men attempt to perform as a group. I pray someone captures this on video.

41

YOU THINK ALIKE

Maddux

I bounce with excitement, standing outside their hotel room. A dumbfounded Christy opens the door.

"Hello," I greet, entering the room.

"What are...you doing here?" she stammers.

As she closes the door, Ryan emerges, freshly showered with wet curls drooping around his face.

"Maddux?" Confusion creases his face.

"I'm here to spend time with my nieces in the most magical place in the world. I plan to entertain them each evening to give you two some honeymoon alone time," I explain. "I secured a room two floors up," I state, sliding a key card into Ryan's hand. "I plan to hang out with the girls this evening. I'll sleep in this adjoining room to keep an eye on them while the two of you spend the night upstairs." I point at the ceiling.

Christy looks at Ryan in wide-eyed disbelief. He shakes my hand as he pats me on the back.

"You are the best brother in the world," Ryan chuckles.

"You will owe me one," I laugh. "Now, off with you. Gather your clothes and toiletries and relocate to the room upstairs. Go."

They quickly grab their clothes from the closet, their suitcase, and items from the bathroom.

Ryan extends his hand to the doorknob, pausing inches away as a knock sounds for the second time in 20 minutes.

"Expecting someone?" Ryan asks Christy.

She shakes her head.

Without looking through the peephole, he swings the hotel door wide open.

"Brooks?" the three of us say in unison.

"Surprise!" Brooks exclaims.

"What are you doing here?" Christy asks, her voice rising an octave.

"I came to be your nanny for the rest of your honeymoon," she announces proudly.

Ryan and Christy exchange glances before looking in my direction.

"Beat ya to it, sweetheart," I taunt the woman in her dark, distressed denim with many rips, leather cuffs, and a Nine Inch Nails tee.

Christy's head whips back to her friend, now inside the room.

Ryan chortles, grabbing his stomach. "I can't believe the two of you had the same idea and arrived on the same day only minutes apart." He points between Brooks and me. "I bet it kills you that you think alike."

"Let's get out of here while we still can," he murmurs, his hand holding a duffle and nudging against Christy's lower back.

"I'll leave it to the two of you to figure out the sleeping arrangements." He laughs before shutting the door.

42

SEPARATE CORNERS AT NIGHT

Brooks

"What are you doing here?" I snap at Maddux.

"Enjoy your time in Florida. I've got this," he states, jutting his chin towards the girls on the nearby bed.

"Uh-uh," I argue. "I didn't come all this way to be alone."

"I'm not sure Ryan and Christy will appreciate you tagging along on their honeymoon," Maddux chuckles.

"Here's a thought. We can watch the girls together," I spit, not liking the amount of venom in my voice.

Maddux opens his mouth to argue, but I stop him.

"We are two reasonable adults. We can play nice for a few days, keep the girls happy, and go to our separate corners at night," I offer.

"There are only two beds," Maddux points out. "I really think it would be frowned upon for me to sleep with my nieces. So, I'll take this room."

Wait a minute! I scan the room I'm standing in. At the window is a desk with an office chair, a lamp, a side table, and a chair. *It is definitely not a recliner.* I frown; there is no hide-a-bed sofa. The thought of sharing a bed with two almost-six-year-olds doesn't thrill me—even if it's a king bed. I know for a fact they kick in their sleep.

"Let's discuss it later," I state, not ready to commit to anything at this time.

Maddux's eyes narrow as he assesses what options I might suggest.

I turn towards the twins. Their attention is fully upon their iPad. "Screen time is over," I announce.

They promptly turn the screen to sleep and place it on the desk. Their eager blue eyes gaze up at me for...*for what? What can we do in this hotel room?* I didn't fully think through my plan to keep them at night, allowing Ryan and Christy alone time.

"What shall we do?" Maddux asks when I grow silent. "We could swim at the hotel pool. We could go out to eat, see a movie, play miniature golf, or go exploring."

Over my shoulder, I stare in disbelief. He one-upped me, he did his research, and he has a plan. I decide to be grateful instead of frustrated.

"What if we swim tonight, order room service, then watch a movie past your bedtime?" he suggests to the girls.

"Yes!" Ry cheers, clapping.

"Will the two of you swim with us?" Harper inquires.

"I brought my suit," I answer, while a smiling Maddux nods.

Maddux

Fate smiles upon me.

Brooks and I will need to share a bed. Granted, my nieces will be in an attached room with the door open. We are both here, and we will share a bed. I'm a lucky man.

I'm done fighting my feelings for her, I'm done avoiding her, and I'm done worrying about Ryan and Christy's opinions where we are concerned. I plan to act upon my feelings. I'm done settling on thoughts of her.

I watch Brooks chat with the girls as they prepare to swim. She ushers them one at a time into the bathroom to pee and put on a swimsuit. Next, Ry and Harper stand at the end of their bed in their swimsuits, flip-flops, goggles, and with toys in hand—eyes glued to the Disney Channel—as Brooks excuses herself to change into her own swimsuit. Once she shuts the bathroom door, I move to put on my own swim trunks.

I imagine Brooks naked mere feet from me. I love her tall frame and tattooed flesh. *I can't wait to touch her... to kiss her... to be with her.* I admonish myself. I can't hide much in my swim trunks with my nieces present. *I must behave. I must wait until the little ones are asleep before I fantasize and act upon my feelings for Brooks.*

Brooks

"Miss Brooks," Harper calls to me from the attached hotel room where she's supposed to be closing her eyes as she attempts to fall asleep for the night.

I peek my head into their room. "Hmm?"

"What's papa-watzy?" she asks.

I arch an eyebrow, realizing she can't see it in the dark room. "Why do you ask?"

"Today at Disney, Daddy told Mommy he saw papa-watzy," Ry adds to our conversation, proving she also struggles to sleep.

"Paparazzi are people with cameras," Maddux answers.

The twins laugh.

Harper speaks. "Everybody at Disney has a camera."

I fight the urge to laugh at the twins, proving Uncle Maddux's answer wrong.

"The paparazzi are people with cameras that take photos of famous people then put them in a magazine or newspaper," I explain.

"And online," Maddux adds.

"Daddy was telling Mommy so they could keep you safe," I theorize. "Sometimes, crowds of other people follow the paparazzi cameras, and it gets crazy."

"Mommy, Daddy, Miss Brooks, and I will all keep you safe from crowds and paparazzi," Maddux states. "You have nothing to worry about; it's our job to keep you safe."

"And have fun," Ry adds.

"Yes. It is our job to make sure we all have fun," Maddux chuckles.

43

2.5 KIDS

Maddux

Our second night in Florida, I decide there will not be two pillows between us in our bed. Tonight, Brooks will need to acknowledge me lying beside her.

"Hmm..." I think out loud.

"What?" Brooks asks from the bathroom vanity.

"Check your texts," I prompt.

I remain propped against pillows, sitting on the bed as I flip through the television channels. I hear rustling from the nearby bathroom and await her reaction to the text. The light flicks off, and she returns to the bedroom with her cell phone in hand.

"Hmm..." she mumbles.

Our eyes meet.

"What will we do with a morning alone?" I ask, hoping she's thinking what I am thinking.

"Did you ask—"

"No," I quickly interrupt. "But I won't refuse a morning off twin duty."

"Hmm..."

I long for her to express more of a reaction. I'd like to know we are on the same page.

"We'll need to get up and help get the girls ready for the beach," Brooks states. "Then…" She lets that word dangle.

"I'm sure we will find something to do," I state, playing it cool.

"Did you find anything?" she asks, gesturing towards the TV on the dresser at the foot of the bed.

"Nah."

Brooks slips under the sheet on her half of the bed. "We could talk," she suggests, rolling onto her side to face me.

Talk? What exactly would we talk about? I've never simply talked to a woman while lying in bed. Surprisingly, I like the idea of talking with Brooks.

I stand, shuck my shorts, flip off the overhead light, and crawl under the blanket. I fidget, unable to find a comfortable position. With an ab crunch, I sit up, removing my T-shirt and tossing it to the floor. I struggled sleeping last night with my T-shirt on. I don't want to spend a second night staring at the ceiling as I listen to Brooks sleep. I contemplated slipping out of my boxers last night, but I worried Brooks would flip out if she happened to see me. I flip to my side, fluff my pillow, and smile at my bed partner.

"Comfy?" she teases.

"I don't normally wear…" I begin to explain.

"You sleep naked…" she says at the same time.

We laugh.

"I'll go first," Brooks chuckles. "I usually sleep in the nude. I locked my door when Christy and the girls lived with me so they wouldn't walk in on me."

Whoa! If she's revealing this much to start with, how deep will this talk get?

"Interesting…" I state, pretending to contemplate her words while I imagine Brooks naked in bed.

I shake away those thoughts and force myself to remain in the moment, listening to all she offers to share.

"Now, it's your turn…" Brooks urges.

"I sleep naked and live alone, so I don't need to lock my bedroom door." I smile nervously, anxious to know if I shared or talked as she expected.

"Tell me something no one knows about you," Brooks urges, tucking her hair behind her ear.

What to share? What to share? Hmmm...

"I feel like the little brother instead of Ryan's older brother," I blurt.

"Really?" she scoffs. "Well, you hide it well. You come across as the accomplished, successful real estate guy, content in his life."

"Perhaps I deserve an Oscar," I jest. "Most days, I'm going through the motions... You know... Dressing the part." I roll my eyes. "Don't get me wrong; I'm good at what I do, I like the money I make, I... I... I'm lonely—less lonely now that Ryan is in KC and Christy and the girls are in our lives. I mean... I own a huge house, but no one lives with me. I'm alone for most meals; I hang out at the club house later than I should, so I don't go home to the empty house. I mean, my mom has been on me for over four years to settle down and start a family, and now on the outside looking in, I want Ryan's family. I want a wife that gets me—that loves me. I want the two-and-a-half kids in the yard and yelling in the house. I'm not sure I'm looking in the right places for...her."

"I believe in fate," she professes.

"No..." I drawl. "You have your special powers." I swirl my finger towards her forehead as I speak.

She gives me a squinty-eyed glare.

"If I had your gift... I'm just saying I would touch the hand of every woman I saw and find Mrs. Right," I explain.

"If you had my gift..." she starts to argue but pauses.

"No. Continue," I urge. "If I had your gift...?"

"It's only cool the first couple of times," she states. "By the time I was ten, I was over the 'gift' and in the 'it's a torture' stage," Brooks declares. "I go to great lengths to avoid all, and I mean all, human contact. I wear two pairs of latex gloves, I don't date, I don't use hook-up apps, I don't..."

"But I am the exception to the rule," I remind her. "I am the exception to all that. You can touch me all you want and no visions."

She nods. *How do I encourage her without scaring her away?*

"I... You're..." she struggles, pursing her lips and closing her eyes for a moment. "You confound me."

Hmm...

"Confound in a good way or...a bad way?"

"I'm not sure." She nervously laughs.

"Let's pretend it's a good way," I suggest, reaching out my left hand to cup her cheek.

I want to say more; I want to encourage her to... *I'm not sure... Of course, she is hot, and I want her. But it...feels... It feels...weird... No. It feels different. She's different. It doesn't escape me that she's giving me the stink eye. She's...she's considering it—she's considering me.*

I have to...

I need us to move on.

"Tell me something about you that no one knows." I toss her question back to her.

"I... My... I don't speak to my parents. I cut them off when I moved out at 21," she shares. "I... Christy knows, but no one else. I had to cut their toxicity from my life. I keep up with my nieces and nephews, but I don't communicate with my parents or my siblings." She cringes, waiting for my reaction.

I ponder this for a moment. At age 21, she cut off all communication with her family. She's Christy's best friend. She rescued her and the twins, allowing them to live with her. She seems like a loyally awesome best friend and adopted aunt for the girls. It's not that she lacks empathy or compassion.

What did her family do to her?

"What if we...?" I point my index finger between us. "What if... You don't have visions..."

She silences my ragged declaration when her mouth collides with mine. Her hands grasp the sides of my head, and she spills... She conveys so much with her kiss.

I follow her lead, cognizant of my nieces in the connected room with the open door between us. Her lips upon mine and her hand to my chest ignites an inferno within me. Never have I reacted to a simple kiss like this. She's not my usual type. In fact, she is so far from my type that she wasn't even on my radar. She's not blonde and modelesque. *Everything about her is chaotic. Not at all my type.* But she's pulling me in, inch by inch. Brooks pulls me from my thoughts.

"The twins," I grunt as she attempts to distracts me.

Her gaze darts over her shoulder through the open door where the girls sleep soundly in the adjoining room. Much to my dismay, she falls to my side, her gaze on the open door and not on me.

Brooks

His reminder is a cold, wet blanket on my libido. Christy left the girls in my—in our—care.

Maddux doesn't seem to... Well, the fact the door is open doesn't stop him. He peppers kisses upon my neck beneath my ear. *We should stop; he should stop, but it feels so good.*

"Madd..." I moan when he sucks on my ear lobe.

I lay, watching the faint nightlight from the girls' room, on my side. My brain tells me we should stop, but my body... My body seeks the power and pleasure his promises to deliver.

"Eyes on the door," he growls.

I nod my understanding and agreement as I continue to cuddle against him.

"Quiet," he orders, and I nod.

I pray for no movement and sound from the adjoining room, as I bask in the warmth of Maddux's arms. Too soon, he releases me, rolling from the bed.

"I need a quick shower," he states, walking across the room.

Odd. I open the Kindle app on my cell phone and begin reading my current paranormal romance novel. Half a chapter in, I believe I hear talking. I crane my neck, trying to ascertain if the twins are up or if there is someone in the hall outside our hotel room. I think it's Maddux in talking in the shower.

I quickly return my attention to my ebook. Minutes later, the shower ceases. When a freshly showered Maddux returns to the bedroom, I pretend to read and not stare at his contoured muscles with a sheen of water coating them.

If...If we weren't on babysitting duty, I would definitely initiate round number two with Maddux.

44

EARTH TO MADDUX

Maddux

Too soon, my alarm signals we need to wake the twins and prepare them for their trip to the beach. Turning my head to the side, I notice Brooks is not beside me. Sitting up, I hear the faint sounds of the shower. I smile, happy she now uses this shower instead of the one in the girls' room.

Since Ryan and Christy will be here any minute, I climb from bed, pulling on my T-shirt and shorts. My toothbrush is in the bathroom with Brooks. I contemplate cracking the door to grab it but don't want to anger her.

"Wakey, wakey, eggs and bakey," I cheer, pulling the blankets off my nieces, eliciting groans. "It's beach day!"

"Uncle Maddux, I'm tired," Harper whines.

"I know, but if you get up and dressed, you won't be," I counter. I realize it doesn't make sense but hope they are too young to see the error in my wisdom.

"You heard mean Uncle Maddux. Get up!" Brooks announces loudly upon joining us.

Of course, the twins listen to her. They crawl off the bed, taking turns in the restroom.

"You were up early this morning." I nudge Brooks's shoulder.

"Well, I didn't take a shower before bed like you did," she says with a hint of a smile.

She knows full well why I needed to shower last night. Perhaps she used the shower noise to cover her need this morning. Hmm... I smirk as the vision fills my thoughts.

"Earth to Maddux," she calls. "Unlock the deadbolt." She points toward the door that leads to the hallway.

"All done!" the twins proclaim.

"Let me inspect," Brooks directs, urging them toward her.

"We brushed our teeth, got dressed, washed our face, and went potty," Ry informs.

"Hand me the hairbrush," Brooks instructs.

"I want Uncle Maddux to do my ponytail," Harper cackles.

Fear floods me; I look to Brooks for assistance.

"Does he know how to make a ponytail?" Brooks inquires.

I shake my head amidst the girls' giggles. "I have no idea how to brush a girl's hair," I state.

"You brush it just like you do your hair," Ry tells me, clearly surprised by my statement.

"I'll style your hair this morning." The twins look from me to Brooks, crossing their arms over their chests. "Then at bedtime, we will teach him how to brush and style your hair." She winks at me, smiling proudly. "You'll have to help them sometime."

I pray she's kidding about teaching me tonight and that I might, someday, need to fix the girls' hair. *Aren't they old enough to style it themselves?*

"Knock, knock," Christy greets, opening the door with Ryan on her heels. "Who's ready for the beach?"

"Me!" Ry and Harper cheer.

"They're all ready," I inform.

Not wasting any time, Ryan urges his family from the room toward the SUV, leaving Brooks and I alone.

"What should we do now?" Brooks inquires, hands upon her hips.

"We could do anything you'd like," I assure her, unsure how to influence her to climb back into bed with me.

"Well..." she drawls, stepping closer to me. "We could..." She fists her fingers in the hem of my T-shirt.

I wet my lower lip as I peer down at her. Her eyes clock the movement. When they return to mine, I find her green orbs full of lust.

I lower my mouth to hers softly at first. I kiss one corner of her mouth before sucking her lower lip tightly between mine. Her eyes widen, and her pupils dilate. I contemplate biting her lip; not knowing her preferences, I decide I'd better not.

45

WHAT'S FOR DESSERT?

Maddux

This... She... I've...
Mind blown.
It's never felt like this. In all my one-night stands, it never felt like this. Any idiot could tell the moment they met Brooks that she is different, but not me.

"Admit it. I'm the best you've ever had," Brooks rasps.
I chuckle. "You know, I was just thinking about that a moment ago."
"And?" she pries, turning on her side toward me.
"I'd like more to compare it to..."
She interrupts. "C'mon!"
I place my index finger over her lips. "If you'd let me finish," I chide. "It was pretty spectacular, I must admit."
"I knew it!" she smugly cheers. "I rocked your world."
Did she ever. I feel like an addict already planning my next hit
"Now, it's your turn to confess," I prompt.
Brooks, flat on her back, stares at the ceiling and doesn't speak.
"You gotta give me something," I beg. "I know I was better than your first time."

I know I rocked her world. I decided to start with probably the worst sex she's ever had, just to get her talking.

"Brooks," I call into the dark room. "Did I do something wrong? Did I hurt you?"

She shakes her head but doesn't throw me a bone, so I prop myself up on my forearm, positioning myself near her. In the pale light from the open doorway, I find Brooks biting her lips together. I must have said something to upset her.

She avoids touch.

She avoids touch, so... Does this mean she's a virgin?

Well, not anymore.

Was she?

I should have been gentle; I should have taken it slow. How did I not consider that she might be a virgin?

"Are...you a virgin?" I murmur, tracing her jawline with my fingertips.

A sweet smile slides upon her lips. "Not anymore."

"I wish I'd known. I could have taken it easy," I apologize.

"Bite your tongue," she scolds. She rolls to face me, placing her palm on my bare chest. "What's for dessert?" she asks.

"I wish I had better news for you," I begin. "I'm out of condoms, so I need to make a trip to a pharmacy before I can serve you dessert."

46

BEING A DAMSEL IN DISTRESS HAS IT'S PERKS

Brooks

My stomach growls loudly in the dark room, causing us to laugh.

"I'd better feed you," Maddux chuckles. "Let's shower."

I arch an eyebrow.

Maddux raises his hands, palms out. "I'm out of condoms. I'm simply suggesting a shared shower."

If I had any reservations about his invitation, his sexy smile and exposed dimple would persuade me to join him. His looks always spark a reaction in me. Recently, his personality has begun pulling me in further. *The two of us hooking up is not a good idea with his connection to the husband of my long-time best friend. When we work through this unfightable attraction to each other, we'll need to overcome the repercussions to keep them from affecting Christy and Ryan as well as the twins.*

I hear the shower spray and the sound of the shower curtain rings sliding against the metal rod. I wait a bit before joining him. I slip between the shower curtain and the tile wall, stepping in with my right foot. When I lift my left leg to completely enter the shower, I'm distracted by the bronze Adonis with water droplets caressing every inch of his toned body. My right foot slips, and I desperately clutch his upper arms. Reflexively, Maddux's hands grasp my hips, steadying me.

Sensing my heart racing and my hands trembling on his arms, he pulls me tight to his slick, soap-covered chest.

His mouth near my ear, Maddux's low, husky voice murmurs, "I've got you."

My breath hitches, and I swoon. *Swoon. I don't swoon. I am not a swooner. Get a grip, Brooks. It feels… It feels amazing to be held by his strong arms.* He saved me from an embarrassing fall. I'm sure I'd be sprawled naked with a head wound had he not caught me. I pride myself on my independence. I will not make a habit of this, but I must admit, being a damsel in distress does have its perks.

My heartbeat continues to race, now due to Maddux's hard body pressed to my soft curves. My fingers relax, and I allow myself to enjoy his arms holding me. I rest my head against his shoulder, the shower spray wetting the top of my head. Slowly, Maddux's hands slide up and down my back.

I should let him know I'm okay, but I allow myself to enjoy this gentle moment.

Maddux

I clutch Brooks to my chest. *She fell into my arms like a woman in a rom-com. I bask in the knowledge I caught her—I rescued her.* I like the feel of Brooks in my arms, against my chest, naked.

As much as I want to stay lost in this moment, we have an important errand to run before Ryan's family returns. I promised her a sexless shower to save time and water. *I should follow through.*

"Want me to wash your back?" I prompt, my gravelly voice.

Brooks turns her head, looking up at me through her wet lashes, crumbling my resolve. I lower my mouth to hers. Without hesitation, her lips mold to mine. She eagerly opens, her tongue darting along my lower lip. It's all the invitation I need.

Wrapping my arm around her abdomen, I pull her tightly against me. Brooks kisses me over her shoulder under the shower spray.

"Let's get clean," she suggests, spinning in my arms.

I place shower gel in the center of a washcloth and lather her shoulders, her back, and her perfect backside.

"A girl could get used to this," she giggles.

A guy could get used to this, too. The more time I spend with her, the more I want to. Everything about Brooks draws me in, leaving me jonesing for more.

47

KEEP IT IN HIS PANTS

Brooks

"You get the condoms. I'll grab some snacks," I suggest as the automatic doors swish open.

Inside CVS we separate, planning to meet at the register in a couple of minutes. I grab two bottles of Diet Pepsi, a bag of chips, and stand in the candy aisle contemplating a sweet snack, when Maddux joins me.

"White chocolate or milk chocolate?" I ask, unable to make the decision on my own.

"White," he immediately answers as he picks up a bag of Payday candy bars.

I grab a bag of white chocolate Reese's and motion toward the registers at the front of the store. As I follow him, I examine the box of condoms in his hand. *He didn't buy a three pack.* Butterflies flutter in my stomach at the thought of all the sex in my future.

At the register, he allows me to place my armful of snacks on the counter before he sits the box of condoms near them. *I quickly read,* "Trojan. Pleasure Pack." Hmm. Interesting. "Variety pack." That sounds fun. "36."

36! Just how much sex does he think we can squeeze in while we babysit? My heart rate increases with many sexy fantasies playing in my mind.

"Brooks," Maddux calls, his hand at the small of my back, urging me toward the exit.

"Holy crap!"

"What?" he asks, his eyes searching my face with concern on his.

"It's Christy," I say, my eyes signaling towards the parking lot.

I snag the bag of snacks from his left hand, leaving the bag with the condoms for him to hide.

"What are you two doing here?" Christy laughs, as she approaches us.

"I needed some munchies," I lie, raising the bag I hold as proof. I pray Maddux has hidden the box of condoms behind me. I don't dare chance a glance.

"What are you doing here?" Maddux asks.

"Harper cut her foot on some coral while we snorkeled," Ry explains, pointing to her twins left foot.

"It's not too bad," Christy assures us. "We're grabbing some antibiotic ointment and bigger bandages."

She shrugs, leading me to believe she's not worried about the injury. I long to touch Harper to see if she will heal quickly or should go to a doctor, but I refrain.

"Did you see us coming to this CVS in a vision?" Ryan asks, now standing by his brother.

I shake my head.

"She was hungry," Harper informs him pointing to my white plastic bag.

"Why don't Maddux and I take the girls back to the hotel, and the two of you shop," Ryan suggests.

"Think you can find your way back?" Maddux asks me.

"I think we can remember how to use the Maps app," I quip.

"Touché," he chuckles.

"Go have your guy time, but keep an eye on the twins until we get back to the room," Christy instructs her new husband.

"Swimming pool! Swimming pool!" the twins chant.

"Absolutely not. There will be no more swimming today. We need to treat your scrape and keep germs off it." Christy orders.

"That means no shower or bath," Harper sasses back.

"Let's go," Ryan laughs, scooping Harper over his shoulder and whisking her to the SUV to protect her from her mother.

Maddux tries to conceal his laughter, but fails miserably. I point towards Ryan, urging him to leave before Christy takes out her anger on him.

"That child," Christy fumes, walking into the store. "I swear she's made it her goal to make me mad all day today."

"So..." I drawl, hoping to take the heat off of Harper. "Other than the scrape, how was the beach?"

"First, did you see what Maddux had in his sack?" Christy turns to face me, hands upon her hips. "He had a box of condoms," she whispers.

Crap! I'm going to kill Maddux. He didn't even try to conceal them.

"Did he meet someone this morning? Did he leave you alone at the hotel all morning? I'm sorry, I should have taken you to the beach with us. I can't believe he couldn't keep it in his pants for my honeymoon."

I snort.

"Rude!" she reprimands.

"I can't help it," I laugh. "You just went on a rant about a guy not having sex on your honeymoon. If anyone is listening, they'll be saying a prayer for your new husband."

Christy huffs, shakes her head, and walks away.

Deflection successful, I follow my best friend, laughing to myself all the way.

48

SECURITY

Maddux

"We have company," Ryan murmurs, glancing into the rearview mirror.

I utilize the passenger-side mirror, spotting a white mid-sized sedan and a blue minivan following us when Ryan strategically changes lanes.

"Paparazzi found us this week at the theme park," he explains. "They took photos from the hoods of their cars at the beach today.

"So, they aren't approaching you or the family?" I question.

"Yesterday, there were only three. Today, there's at least six," Ryan complains, taking an exit near our hotel.

"The word has spread," I state the obvious. "Once photos hit social media and websites, paparazzi and vacationers will all scramble for a photo."

"When we get in the room, can you distract the girls while I arrange security?" My brother implores.

"Of course," I immediately respond. "You should know the twins asked Brooks and I last night what paparazzi were. They heard you mention them to Christy yesterday."

"A side effect of my job; the girls will learn to remain aware of their presence as they ignore them," Ryan states, looking briefly at his daughters in the back seat.

At the same time, our eyes spot the crowd gathered at the hotel's entrance.

"They found us," he groans.

"Um Daddy," Ry scorns.

"Swear jar," Harper cheers.

"Ry and Harper," I call into the backseat of the SUV as I turn to face them. "A crowd is here with cameras like we talked about last night. Stay in your seats until we help you out."

Ryan parks near the valet station. No sooner in park, he turns to face his daughters. "Unbuckle and slide towards Ry's door," he directs. "Uncle Maddux and I will open your door and carry you inside."

The twins nod in understanding, Ryan looks to me, I nod, and we exit opposite sides of the vehicle. I wait for him to wave at his fans before I open the back door. We each scoop up a girl and briskly enter the hotel lobby. Once inside the heavy glass doors block out the adoring fans, hoping for a brief interaction with the NFL athlete.

"Ry and Harper, hold Uncle Maddux's hand. He'll take you up to our room. I need to talk to the hotel staff before I come up. 30 minutes of screen time, after you change from your swimsuits and wash your hands," he instructs.

"Screen time until Brooks and Mommy return," Ryan announces before he closes the hotel room door behind him. "You in there," he orders, pushing me into my hotel room.

He waits at the door, eye on the twins until their full attention is back on the iPad.

"Spill," he demands.

My brow furrows.

"You bought condoms," he states.

I shrug, scrambling for an explanation.

"A bunch of condoms," he whisper-yells. "How many women did you meet this morning?"

I chuckle, relieved he doesn't suspect I plan to use every one of them with Brooks. I'm not ready for his lecture where Brooks is concerned.

"Brooks needed snacks, and I realized I didn't pack any just in case I met someone," I lie. "You know me, I need to be prepared."

"So, do you sneak out at night when the twins fall asleep?" he asks, too eager for my answer.

I shake my head. "Just putting a couple in my pocket in case something pops up while we are out."

"Pops up alright," he laughs. "Don't let Christy see them. She'll lecture you on keeping it in your pants around your nieces."

"I promise I'll be on my best behavior around Ry and Harper," I vow, crossing my heart with my index fingers.

49

STUPID BABY BROTHER

Brooks

Arms full of plastic grocery bags, we make our way from CVS to the rental vehicle.

"Crap!" Christy barks. "They didn't all follow Ryan and the girls."

I scan the parking lot, noting two telephoto lenses on cameras pointed at the two of us. They click pictures over and over, documenting our every step to and as we load the back seat.

"Can you text Maddux and Ryan that we are on our way back? We might need their help unloading if the paparazzi swarms us. Because the wedding photos were published, it seems even our random honeymoon photos are in high demand," Christy thinks aloud as we follow directions from the Maps App back to the hotel.

Until this summer, I've enjoyed the photos and videos professional photographers sold to entertainment sites and publications. Now I see they sometimes invade privacy to get the shots I greedily consumed. Ryan and Christy handle it well, while all I want to do is punch them then take a baseball bat to their giant cameras.

"Frickety, frick, frick, frack." I don't believe my eyes. It seems like one hundred fans swarm the barricades along the sidewalk to the entrance of our hotel. Scattered amidst them large, black, zoom lenses protrude over the metal bars.

Christy reads her cell phone before we exit, "Ryan says to wait at valet until the security guys open our doors to escort us inside."

"This is insane," I marvel.

"It's part of our daily lives now," she grumbles.

And mine by association. I need to ask Ryan and Christy for hints on how to ignore them and go about my life as if they are not there. I'll never be a natural at it like they are, but surely, I can learn not to want to punch them.

A heavy fist knocks on Christy's window. He opens the driver's door at the same time another burly guy opens mine. They usher us swiftly into the hotel and the safety of the elevator, escorting us all the way into our room. I can't help but wonder how crazy the amusement parks will be tomorrow.

"Come here you," Ryan calls to his new bride. His eyes shift to me as he holds Christy snug to his chest. "They didn't get too close, did they?"

I shake my head. "How'd you hire security so quick?"

"My publicist wanted me to allow the security detail to start shadowing us at our wedding," Ryan "I insisted we wait until…"

"Until they intruded today," Maddux jumps in teasing. "I still can't believe anyone is interested in my stupid baby brother."

"You said the 'S' word!" Harper points out.

"Swear jar!" Ry orders, pointing to her uncle.

I carry the red and gold, Cardinals gallon container the girls decorated toward him. "That's a dollar, Uncle Maddux."

We enjoy a laugh as he mumbles, his fingers fiddling for a dollar bill in his money clip. They've already emptied its contents once and made a trip to their bank with the proceeds.

"The two of you should head upstairs," Maddux suggests, sparing me a quick look. "Miss Brooks can conduct bath time, and I can handle bedtime."

"If you're sure," Christy says through a yawn.

"Off with you," I order, pointing to the door.

"We'll meet with the security detail and share the plan with you in the morning," Ryan offers, standing in the open doorway.

Beyond him I see a security man watching our doors. *I wonder if he'll be posted there overnight.*

50

HE HAD ONE JOB

Brooks

At the sound of the door latching, I announce, "Bath time!"

The twins scramble for pajamas, undress, and climb into the tub before Brooks has it ready. She kneels at the tub's edge, making quick work of covering them in suds from head to toe and rinsing them off.

"Two-minute warning," I declare, retreating to the safety of the outer room to avoid the splashes.

"I still can't believe that works." Maddux shakes his head. Leaning over my shoulder, he murmurs for only me to hear. "I can't wait for them to fall asleep."

Spinning to face him, I place a hand upon his chest. "Easy tiger," I tease. "They are pretty high strung; it will probably take hours to put them to sleep tonight." I laugh out loud at his wide-eyed reaction. *Someone's got the thirty-six pack of condoms on his mind.*

Maddux dries the bathroom floor while I tuck the girls in and read them a bedtime story. While they are seeming more tired than I thought earlier, they do wait for Maddux to read them a second story before I shut off the lights and they close their eyes.

"I've got twenty dollars for the first one to fall asleep," Maddux bribes, urging them to sleep.

In our adjoining room, I gather my sleep set and begin washing my face.

"Bribery won't work," I mumble as I scrub my cheeks.

"What?" Maddux laughs.

I guess I did mumble unintelligibly. I remove the facial cloth from over my mouth before repeating myself, "Bribery won't work." I look at the large man towering over me in my reflection. "Do you mind?" *I don't need him watching me remove my makeup and moisturize.*

He pats me on my butt. "Hurry up."

Hurry up? We can't...Surely, he knows that the twins aren't deep asleep yet. When I return to my task, I find I grin like a schoolgirl in the mirror. I zip through my routine and slip into my tank and shorts for the night. I find the room dark but for Maddux's cell phone screen where he lays on our bed under the covers. My belly flutters as thoughts of what he's wearing, or not wearing, come to mind. *I mean just because the twins aren't sound asleep doesn't mean we can't start to fool around a bit.*

Maddux flips my side of the sheet back, inviting me to climb in beside him, and I quickly abide.

My mind on the security man in the hallway, I say the first thing that I think of to fill the silence. "It will be weird with a security team everywhere we go tomorrow." I look to him for confirmation.

"I imagine the girls will be excited running from ride to ride. Hopefully we can focus on them and not the bulky, lineman-looking dudes glued to our group." He attempts to make light of my worries and the reason we need security in the first place. "Are you worried for their safety?"

His question causes me pause. *It feels awkward to need adult men to lurch nearby, and I don't like the cameras pointed in our direction. But I don't feel we are in danger. Maybe if Ryan and Maddux weren't so tall and full of muscles, I'd fear the fans.* I shake my head in answer to his question.

"We can give them nicknames and try to make them smile all day," he suggests.

I like that idea, and the twins might get a big kick out of it. Uncle

Maddux is grasping his new uncle duties with a flourish. I rest my head upon his shoulder and absent-mindedly trail my fingers slowly down his bare chest.

"Do you think any photos are already..." I'm interrupted.

"Ryan's publicist gets alerts for any photos and comments," Maddux informs me. "She shared a few with Ryan that already hit social media. There's one she's concerned she might need to track down and get removed."

"Really? Is it bad?" I scramble for anything that might have happened at the beach, hotel or CVS to cause... "Noooo!"

"Shh," Maddux scolds. "We are trying to get the twins to sleep not wake them up."

"The condoms?" I whisper, dreading his response.

"Yep," he nods as he replies. "The photographer zoomed in, and you can read the box through the plastic bag. So far no one has alluded to them being Ryan and Christy's."

Why didn't he hide them? He let Ryan and Christy easily see them, and now the entire world. Gah! He should have tucked them under his shirt or in another bag. He had one job!

"I'm not... I never... I've never had to hide my purchase before. Ryan saw the condoms but didn't know they were for the two of us," he points his finger between us as he speaks. "In one of the photos, you can see the box of condoms clearly through the bag in my hand. That's no big deal, except..."

"Except you are carrying one of the twins, and Ryan does the same beside you," I finish for him.

"It sucks they can't even take a family vacation without cameras everywhere they look," he grumbles before placing sweet kisses down my neck over my shoulder.

Instantly, my focus shifts fully to the man beside me. I close my eyes, allowing Maddux's hands to move along my ribs to my hips, over my shirt and sleep shorts.

51

MADDUX THE MAGNIFICENT

Maddux

I'm torn between watching Brooks float down from bliss and spotting any sign of movement from Ry and Harper. *How do parents find time to be intimate while raising kids? My parents figured out how to slip in sex or I'd be an only child.*

The thought of my parents having sex, sends a full body tremor through me.

Brooks giggles at my side. "What was that for?"

I can't tell her my true thoughts. I scramble for a plausible reason. "I was shaking away the worry that your scream of pleasure woke the twins," I fib.

Brooks eyes grow wide. "I screamed?" Her hand flies to her mouth in horror.

Brooks rolls to face me. "You...um..." she stammers. "You are a magician."

A magician, huh? Maddux the magician—I like that. Maddux the magnificent—even better.

If Brooks's didn't cause the girls to stir, I assume they are sound asleep. I slide from beneath the sheet, moving the door within an inch of closing. I peek through the crack. In the faint light of the nightlight, I spy the twins sleeping like starfish upon their bed. I hurry to join Brooks for another round.

Our ragged breathing seems to echo off the walls, and our chests rise and fall rapidly.

Brooks's jaws relax, freeing the skin at my shoulder. "Sorry," she giggles, wiping away her slobber.

It hurts even with her teeth removed. It will leave a mark. *I've been marked.* I like the idea of being marked by Brooks.

Aware I'm squishing her, I roll onto my back. Our arms are side by side, and our fingers touch. Our breaths even out.

"Tomorrow will be a crazy day," she whispers.

I turn my head towards her.

"I suspect there will be tons of cameras at the amusement park," she explains. "I've never flown in a private jet, so I'm a little worried about that."

"I've been on small jets for business and with Ryan before," I share. "I think you will like it more than flying commercial. It's more relaxing at the airport and during the flight."

I snake my arm over her midsection and tug her into me. Her bare back tight to my chest, I rest my head upon hers, my mouth near her ear.

"I don't want us to end," I confess into the dark room.

"We promised..." she begins to argue.

"I will keep my promise if that is what you still want," I vow. I bury my nose in her hair and inhale. "I want more of you. I've never... I don't..."

Brooks

"You don't hook up multiple times with the same woman," I finish for him.

A heavy anvil sinks to the bottom of my stomach. *I knew this. I knew what Maddux Harper was like before I ever agreed to have sex with him. Hell, I even suspected I'd get hurt in our weeklong tryst, but I went for it anyway. He is my one chance at sex without having visions, so I told myself it would be worth the hurt to experience a real man in my bed. Now that it is time to end, I want to cling to him and never let him go.*

"We could..." he pauses before finishing his thought.

We could... We could? We could date. We could continue sneaking around. We could give us a try. What could we do?

"I want to keep seeing you when we return to Missouri," he states, finding his words.

I lean up on one forearm, looking closely at his face in the faint light of our room. I search for sincerity.

"You're Ryan's brother and I'm Christy's friend," I remind him. "We will see each other." My heart is heavy in my chest. I cannot imagine only seeing each other in their presence.

"I want more than that," Maddux shares. "I want to be alone with you. I want to hold you. I want you."

He didn't say to date.

"What will we tell Ryan, Christy and the girls?" I seek further explanation from him. I am desperate to know what he wants. *Is he hoping to be a couple or friends with benefits?*

"I've never wanted... I've never done this... I'm not sure if I can do it, but I want to keep what we have here in Florida going back in Missouri," he explains.

"So, you want to keep sneaking around?" I ask.

"I don't like the sneaking, but I don't want to hurt my family," he says, placing his palm to my cheek.

He's not offering to date me, he's not offering to be more than a booty call, but he is offering to spend time alone with me like this-- touching. It is more than I'd ever thought I would have.

I've kept a secret from most of the world my entire life. What is one more secret?

52

COVER STORY, COVER STORY

Maddux

As we take off, Ryan nudges my shoulder from his seat next to mine. "Things get a little rough last night?" Ryan asks low.

My brow furrows. I look to him unsure what he means.

"Teeth marks on your shoulder," her murmurs, smirking.

I school my features, wanting to throw my head back in exasperation. I thought my sleeves would cover it. *Come up with a cover story. Come up with a cover story.* My brain scrambles this way and that.

"I bet Brooks gave you crap for sneaking out to get laid," my brother chuckles.

My eyes dart around the cabin, praying Christy and Brooks are not listening.

"Silence. I get it," Ryan says, nudging me again. "Christy would kill me if you shared any details. She doesn't want your tomcat ways to corrupt me."

Did I just get off without muttering a single word?

For the rest of our private jet flight home, I force myself to listen to Ryan as he shares his dream of running a sports academy in his retirement. I enjoy spending time with my brother and his family, but my

Brooks

thoughts drift the entire flight to Brooks sitting near the sleeping twins. I long to pull out my phone to text her, but Ryan would see.

When the landing gear, connects with the runway, I breathe a little easier, knowing I will soon be out from under Ryan's watchful eyes. I help Harper slip on her backpack before grabbing my own. As we walk from the jet, I pull my cell phone from my back pocket, immediately scrolling to Brooks in my texts.

> ME
> my place or yours?

I press send and fear envelopes me. I've sent many a hookup message, but it feels dirty sending one to Brooks. *She's...different.* It's not a one-night stand text. It's not a once-a-month message to hookup. Brooks is different, and I fear my text belittles what we have. My thumb hovers over my screen as my family climb into the large, black SUV waiting on the tarmac for us, when my phone vibrates with a text.

> BROOKS
> yours?

I breathe a sigh of relief that she didn't say 'not tonight.' I've never worried a hookup might say no. I never cared enough—until now.

The twins occupy the third-row seats, while Brooks, Christy, and Ryan take the middle bench seat. I climb into the front passenger seat, cell phone still in hand. I glance over my shoulder to ensure Ryan and Christy cannot see my phone screen before I text.

> ME
> garage code 7878

Before I press send, I realize Christy sits by Brooks and will be able to read any texts she receives, so I wait until we drop her off at her apartment before my thumb presses send.

> **ME**
> pull into garage
> & pack a bag

My insides warm at the thought of Brooks spending an entire night at my place. I'm almost giddy. That thought causes me pause. I've never allowed a hookup to see my house; I had rules keeping my life private from the random women. Only my family and close golfing buddies ever visit my house—until now. *Brooks is coming over.*

53

PLANT GUY

Brooks

I enter the gate code as I do each time, I visit Christy and Ryan's house. However, this time I turn much earlier into Maddux's drive. I look to our texts and quickly enter the garage code into the keypad. I find myself glancing around, hoping no neighbors see. If one person saw us, they could tell Ryan or Christy.

I jog back to my car, pulling into the safety of Maddux's garage. I turn off the ignition, hoping to collect myself before I exits, but he presses the button on the garage wall to close the door. My head jolts in his direction, finding him leaning against the doorframe, arms crossed over his chest, still wearing the black Disney t-shirt the twins chose for him. My hand trembles, opening the car door.

"Welcome," Maddux greets, hurrying down to take my bag from me.

"How chivalrous," I tease, laughing nervously.

"Let me show you around," he says entering the house. "This is my kitchen, over there is the living room, and there, of course…"

"Is the dining room," we say in unison.

I look around the space, shocked at his décor. Fresh herbs grow in the kitchen window, a potted palm towers near the large doors and windows to the back yard area, and other smaller houseplants scatter throughout the space. He's a bachelor with a hectic work schedule and frequent golf matches, but he has plants that require constant attention to continue to grow. I make a note to talk to him about his abundance of plants later.

A navy and green color scheme continues through window treatments, furniture, and accents as he shows me the theater room, pool and patio area, his office, and the bedrooms. His lower-level game room, however, is an explosion of red, gold, and all things KC Cardinals. Most of the items depict football and Ryan, but he also has KC Cardinals baseball, soccer, and basketball items sprinkled in. I almost feel like I'm in a local sports bar instead of a basement of a private residence.

"This is quite a house for a single guy," I chuckle on our way back upstairs.

"I mean it is bigger than your apartment..."

"You think?" I scoff. "My entire apartment fits in your living room, kitchen, and dining room."

He shrugs off my comment. "I work in commercial real estate; my house is a reflection of my business."

He places his hand atop mine on the back of a kitchen stool. "What would you like to drink?"

My eyes meet his baby blues. I want to tug him down the hallway, pushing him down on his ginormous bed. *A drink is the last thing on my mind, but if I want to be more than a friend with benefits, I need treat our time together as such.*

"What do you have?" I ask, looking for direction.

"Paul keeps my place stocked," Maddux shares, walking to the refrigerator. "I have water, juice, diet pop, milk..."

"Maddux," I interrupt laughing, fearing he might list every liquid item in this giant house.

He bends, looking toward the wine fridge under the kitchen island. "In here is beer, red and white wine, or I have a fully-stocked bar downstairs," he continues.

"So, you have anything I crave," I restate with a smirk. "What are you having?"

Maddux returns to my side of the kitchen island. "I'll be having you," he murmurs, dropping his lips to caress mine.

His kisses me slow and long. His words during our first time together come to mind. I press on his chest. "I'll be dessert."

His blue eyes widen. "I should feed you supper," he realizes.

"We should eat. Yes," I laugh.

"Paul left me grilled chicken with chimichurri sauce," Maddux informs, opening the fridge door to show me.

"And Paul is...?"

"He runs my house for me. You know Paul," he claims. "He's Josh's partner."

My mind scurries to work out the meaning. "Josh? Like Ryan and Christy's Josh?" *How did I not know this?*

Maddux sits the dish of grilled chicken on the counter before bending over in laughter. *Rude.*

"You really didn't know?" he asks as his laughter subsides, and I shake my head.

"Paul's worked for me over five years now. When Ryan moved into his penthouse downtown, Paul introduced Josh to him." Maddux sets a container of green chimichurri next to the chicken. "They weren't quite dating at the time, but it wasn't long before they did. When Ryan decided to build his house down the road, the two were ecstatic to be working next door to each other so they could carpool."

"Wow, that is convenient." I walk toward the food, preparing to help Maddux heat it up.

Maddux looks to his cell phone for direction. "He says to warm it in the oven or slice and eat cold."

I press buttons on the lower oven. "I prefer warm chicken," I state.

"What do you drink with chicken?" Maddux asks me. "I can do wine or beer."

"Beer's great," I answer.

Maddux rattles off several beers to choose from, and I tell him I'll have what he has. Together we warm the chicken and vegetables that Paul previously grilled, top them with chimichurri, making a colorful dish that we consume on the kitchen stools. The kitchen tasks calm my nerves.

Between bites, I decide to learn more about the man I'm sleeping with. "So…"

"Yes…" he drawls imitating me.

"Does Paul do everything Josh does for Ryan and Christy?" I ask.

Maddux quickly chews his recent bite and washes it down with a swig of his beer. "Paul does everything. He keeps me organized, runs my house, and cleans."

My eyebrows arch at the last task.

Maddux understands my surprise. "Josh has an aversion to cleaning. You should hear Paul give him crap about it. Ryan had to agree to hire a cleaning staff before he hired Josh." He shrugs. "I'm luckier than my brother. Paul does it all."

He sets me up perfectly for my next question. "So, Paul's a plant guy then?"

Maddux tilts his head and his brow furrows as he attempts to understand my meaning. I motion my hand through the space at all the green foliage.

"I'm not sure if Paul's a plant guy, but he helps keep my plants alive, so he isn't a plant-killer," he laughs.

"You…like…plants?"

Maddux quirks his mouth to one side. "They clean the air in a space, they add a pop of color, and…" His sexy smirk and dimple slide upon his face, and he nods. "I'm a plant guy."

"I love it," I smile. "It was a great surprise. I had you pegged as living in a true bachelor pad. Your house like you can be deceiving."

"Good deceiving, I hope," he says, his next forkful poised near his mouth.

"It's all good," I promise, swirling my hands around the open-living space.

Maddux

"Done?" I ask, jutting my chin towards Brooks's plate.

She nods and I carry our plates to the sink. I place another beer in front of her before I rinse our plates and utensils then sit them in the dishwasher. Unable to allow me to do all the work, Brooks carries our empty beer bottles to the recycle bin.

"Now what?" she queries, hands upon her hips.

My eyes narrow, assessing her. Does she want me to say 'dessert', or would she like to hang out for a while? Flashbacks to high school and the first year of college dates come to mind. When I moved from dates to hookups, I did away with this uncertainty and the uncomfortable moments.

"I chose the beer; you tell me," I challenge.

"Let's listen to music and talk for a while," she nonchalantly suggests.

I wonder if she's as uncomfortable as I am with this pre-sex stuff.

"We should let our food digest a bit before heavy exercise," she quips.

Heavy exercise. I like the way she thinks. *There won't be little girls in the next room tonight. We may be unrestrained; I can't wait to experience that with Brooks.*

Should I? I close my eyes several scenarios flooding through my mind. Screw it. I rise, briskly walking down the hall. I lean my shoulder against the wall, crossing my feet and arms, hoping to look calmer than I am.

Brooks emerges from the restroom distracted eyes on her phone and bumps into me.

"Oh!" Her wide green eyes bounce everywhere.

I don't speak; I don't wait. My hands clutch her shoulders an instant before my mouth slams to hers. Brooks stands frozen for a bit, before melting into my body, and her mouth reciprocating my kiss. Her hands press on my back, clinging tightly to me. When she nips at my lower lip, I open, allowing her tongue to meet mine. Our heads move to one side then the other, allowing us to open wider and consume more of each other. Our teeth clank, but we do not stop. We're sloppy, we're hungry, and we're greedy.

Gasping for breath, Brooks pulls away, resting her forehead on my shoulder.

"Time for dessert," I proclaim, lifting her fireman-style over my shoulder and carrying further down the hall. For the first time in my life, I take a woman to my bed.

54

BLUE BALLS

Brooks

"You know the last time I rode a cart around the course, I caused quite a stir," I chuckle upon entering Christy's kitchen, the second Saturday in August.

"Whoa, look at you," Josh says, eyes like saucers at my appearance. "They won't dare post about you today."

"Wow, Brooks," Ryan's voice is heavy with shock. "You look like a real golfer."

"A real golfer"... You have no idea. Today will be a shock for all of them. I've kept a very big secret.

"Let's go," I encourage.

"We're waiting on Maddux," Ryan informs me.

"He has a cart and knows his way to the clubhouse," I remind my friends, playing like I still can't stand the man.

"Ryan plans to ride on Maddux's cart," Christy states. Her eyes urge me not to make a big deal about it.

"Then, we should ride our cart to his house," I suggest, not wanting to stand around listening to my friends ooo and ahh over my attire.

I'm climbing onto Christy's golf cart when Maddux pulls into the driveway. Us ladies head for the clubhouse while Ryan quickly moves his golf paraphernalia onto his brother's golf cart. Christy and I load our cooler with beers, waters, and tons of ice. By the time we exit the clubhouse, the guys are parked by our cart.

"Ready?" Christy asks, back in the driver's seat.

"As ready as I'll ever be," I reply.

At the first tee box, Maddux and Ryan tease each other about attire, practice swings, and club choice. Ryan's drive lands five feet to the right of the fairway. Maddux drives the ball twenty yards farther in the center of the fairway, sparking more teasing as they return to the cart. Christy moves our cart up to the women's gold tees, and we select our drivers from our bags. I encourage Christy to hit first. She draws her club back, swings through, and her ball soars through the cloudless blue sky, landing on the left side of the fairway.

"Great shot, honey," Ryan praises.

"Thanks," she smiles proudly. Turning back to me, she encourages, "Take your time. We're golfing for fun today."

I want to respond with something witty that alludes to my hidden golf skills. I draw a blank and decide to focus on my first swing of a club in five years. I tee my blue golf ball high in front of the head of my driver, I shift my weight through my hips, and adjust my grip. I exhale, draw my club forward connecting solidly with my ball. Ting. My blue Titleist ball flies in a high arc, down the center of the fairway even with Ryan's ball.

"Holy crap!" Maddux scoffs. "Brookie has been holding out on us."

My nickname on Maddux's lips sounds like velvet. *Who would have thought I'd like him using it?*

"You little... you... I can't believe you didn't..." Christy struggles. Excitement and hurt war within her.

"I might have played on the high school golf team in a former life," I explain. "It's a no-contact sport. And my family belongs to the Milburn Country Club."

The three of them openly gawk at me.

"Yo, let's play," I suggest, motioning for them to move toward our balls.

"Today's round just became more interesting," Maddux chuckles. "Let's couples' scramble."

My entire body stiffens at the word couples. I fear Christy and Ryan might read into it. I need to step up my nit-picking on Maddux to ensure we seem at each other's throats and not hooking up.

"I don't plan on losing," I declare in Maddux's direction. "So you better bring you're A-game."

"We've got this," he assures me with a wink.

Why did he wink? That doesn't deflect any speculation.

"Game on," Christy accepts the challenge. "On the cart we are friends; on the course we are competition."

Maddux was right; today's outing just got interesting.

Christy and Ryan's second shot lands on the fringe of the green. I drop my ball by Maddux's, preparing for a one-hundred fifty-yard approach shot.

"Aren't you full of secrets," Maddux murmurs low with a sexy smirk.

"You like that I shock you," I tease, shifting my hips as I address my ball.

A growl emanates from Maddux's chest. I love that I'm torturing him.

My friends expect me to play well today despite my many years away from the game. I study the shot, opt to club up one iron, and send my ball onto the green.

"Holy hell," Maddux cheers. "What iron was that?"

I extend my club face of my five-iron toward him.

"Nice shot Brookie," Christy greets me back on our cart as we motor towards the green. "Maddux and you are going to obliterate us," she grumbles.

"I haven't played in five years. There's no way I will put together a solid round," I assure her. "I'm very out of practice."

"Whatever," she scoffs.

We birdie hole one, par two and three, bogey four, par five and six, birdie seven, bogey eight, and par number nine. We finish even, and Christy's team does the same. The men aren't happy with a tie, but Christy and I are happy we played well.

"Got another nine in you," Ryan asks.

"What do you say, Brooks?" Maddux looks to me hopeful.

"You just want to see me play with my blue balls for another nine," I taunt.

I look at my best friend.

When she nods, I agree, "Let's do this."

"You've waited nine holes to use the blue balls comment, didn't you?" Christy laughs back at the cart.

I wink at my friend.

55

PRYING EYES

Maddux

"Bro!" Ryan's voice is much too loud for the golf course. "You've been holding out on me."

Now what?

He points to his cell phone in the holder on the steering wheel. I lean over, noticing *The Back 9 Talk* post fills his screen. I slip my own phone from my back pocket, pulling up the blog in my Instagram feed. I read through the post.

The Back 9 Talk--8/20

Garages attempt to hide late-night booty calls.
Often empty for weekly business trips, a garage spot in the Pyke Place neighborhood hides a new blue vehicle on a regular basis.
While the cat's away the mice do play.
Breakstone Cliffs residents, your gates don't make you immune. A

neighbor often allows a certain guest to park hidden behind the closed garage door.
Your actions might be private, but the prying eyes of your neighbors see all.
One wonders, is it appropriate to give your late-night tryst a garage door remote of their own?

Not believing what I'm reading, I read it a second time.

Who the hell writes this? I assume it's a woman. *Where and how does she know all this? She can't live in both neighborhoods. She has to have lots of "little birdies" keeping her posted at the club.*

"You think this is me?" I fake offense, pointing to my phone screen.

"I think one of your one-night stands got her hooks into you, and you've allowed her to come to your house," Ryan claims. "Admit it; you've fallen for someone. Christy and I've noticed a change in you lately."

My eyes narrow in his direction. *A change? No way...Have I really changed lately?*

"Dude, I'm just yanking your chain," Ryan laughs.

I laugh it off. Or at least I try to laugh it off convincingly.

Maddux

The Back 9 Talk—9/15

Crime is on the rise at the club. Teenagers up to no good and a thief have neighbors installing more security cameras.
Local law enforcement claims to be working overtime, cracking down on crime in our community. Pranksters, poker cheats, and thieves be warned

My iPhone alerts multiple incoming texts. Turning it over, I swipe the screen to life.

> **WADE**
> did you see it?
>
> **ROBERTO**
> what's up with new rumor?
>
> **WADE**
> I think it's time to take a hiatus
>
> **STEVE**
> I doubt it's about us

My thumbs hover, while I attempt to organize my thoughts. *"poker cheats"… "law enforcement"… "working overtime"… "in our community"*

We are not active in our community. We avoid poker games at the club. We might pop in to see who's there, but we don't play. It's not about us; it can't be. We're vigilant to fly under the radar.

> **ME**
> don't get your panties in a bunch
>
> we're careful
>
> it's not about us
>
> **ROBERTO**
> we continue as planned
>
> **WADE & STEVE**
> (thumbs up emoji)

It's at times like these I remind myself we're doing good. We're robbing from multi-millionaires at illegal poker games and giving the funds to those in need. We've syphoned millions into many respectable charities. I delude myself; I'm breaking the law. If uncovered, my deeds would hurt Ryan's reputation and his family. I'm not sure how Brooks might react to my gambling deeds. *She perplexes me.* Every time I believe I have a hint of figuring her out, she proves I have not the foggiest idea. I hope she might understand why I do what I do. I'd like to think she might support my actions. *I want her to know there's more to me than business suits and golf. I want her to know every part of me.*

Several more texts arrive from my guys. They won't feel safe until we talk in person.

> ME
> my place ten tonight

By ten-thirty, I've successfully calmed the nerves of my crew. We're talking sports when we hear it. We freeze, eyes alert, and ears preened toward the garage. Slowly the sound of my garage door opening then closing announces an unwelcome visitor. Only Ryan, Christy, and Brooks know my garage code. I hold my breath waiting for Brooks or my brother to enter. I remain quiet, formulating my lie to cover up our meeting.

I watch as the door slowly opens and Brooks steps through. Her large green eyes fear her unannounced arrival is unwelcome.

"Hey," she offers low and nervous. "Sorry I'm interrupting."

"Nonsense," Wade says. "The more the merrier."

Brooks's eyes look to me for assurance.

"The guys and I were plotting a real estate endeavor," I lie.

"I didn't see any cars in the driveway," she apologizes for her intrusion.

"We don't like to buzz in at the front gate, so we park and walk in,"

Roberto explains. "You must be Brooks. Maddux talks about you all the time."

What. The. Hell? I do not talk about her "all the time". I warned them once about her gift, and they needed to stay on the opposite side of the room from her.

"Has he?" she drawls, a smile forming.

"All good things," Roberto states. "I'm Roberto by the way." He extends his hand to shake hers.

Idiot.

I breathe a sigh of relief when Brooks waves at him.

"I'm Wade, and he's Willie. You'll have to ignore Roberto. He can't help but flirt with pretty ladies. Wade place his arm on Roberto's shoulders pulling him farther away from Brooks.

At least he remembered to stay far from her.

"We're done, so we'll get out of the way." Wade smirks. "You kids have fun."

Awkwardly the three men exit into the garage, neglecting to shut the door completely behind them. Now alone, I worry what questions Brooks might ask.

56

I THOUGHT I LOST YOU

Brooks

I place my hand on the door, closing it the final four inches, with a multitude of questions swirling in my head. I startle when a man's hand wraps around the door, connecting with mine. With visions playing, I barely see Willie's head peek in or hear his apology for not closing the door in the first place.

Two visions of Willie assault me. One seems to be the past, a trial, law enforcement, and him signing paperwork. In the other vision, Willie's visited by a plain-clothed officer, discussing his new identity and ensuring his continued anonymity.

Willie's not really Willie.

When the fog of the visions clears, Maddux stands between me and the closed door, concern upon his face.

"Everything okay?" he asks, hands moving to my shoulders.

I smile up at him. "My surprise is not going as planned," I admit. "You said you had a work thing until late, so I planned to be here waiting for you when you arrived home."

Maddux awards my favorite smile. His dimple and his blue eyes shine.

"I'm sorry, I..." he silences me with his kiss.

I'm not sure if it's a distraction or he's truly glad I popped by tonight. I'm distracted by my visions of Willie; I'm sure he might sense it in my kiss.

"I love your surprises," he declares with a husky voice, his thumb swiping along my lower lip.

"Do you hold business meetings at home often?" I inquire.

His mouth quirks at the corner, and he shakes his head. "We had to meet later to fit into everyone's schedule tonight," he explains.

"Willie seems like a good guy," I state, setting myself up to ask questions.

"They are all good guys," he states.

"How long have you known him?" I ask.

Maddux's eyes search mine. "Did you have a vi... vision?"

I nod.

"What was he doing?" he asks on high alert.

"I saw him in trouble," I share. "There were flashes of court proceedings, law enforcement, then him signing paperwork."

Maddux's eyes close tight and he sighs deeply.

"I didn't mean to touch..." I defend at the same time Maddux states, "I need to tell you about my guys."

His tone leads me to believe he knows about Willie, and maybe he's involved. I school my features, not wanting to cast judgement.

"I'm not sure how you'll take it," he mutters. "Hell, you've probably already seen most of it."

He thinks I saw him in my vision. I should tell him what I saw, but I really want to know what he is about to confess.

"I know it's against the law, but we do it for good causes," he explains. "We're not hurting anyone that..."

I place my hand on his forearm. "Maddux tell me from the beginning."

"We attend underground poker games and donate our winnings to charity," he states rapidly, his eyes searching my face for my reaction.

"So... you attend illegal poker games and donate your winnings," I restate. *That doesn't seem too bad. In my vision I saw Willie in court, so maybe they were arrested.*

"We don't win," he hedges. "We cheat to win."

Hmm.

"You act like Robin Hood then," I state. "You rob from the rich criminals and give it to the needy."

"I guess that's right," he answers. "No one knows but my crew."

"And now me," I surmise.

"Now that you know..." he can't finish the question.

"Why do you...How did you decide to target the underground poker games?" I inquire.

"We were fed up with super wealthy men snubbing people at the club, not holding doors for people, not offering to carry items for elderly woman... it cost nothing to be courteous. We were all complaining about it, just spouting off really. It worked Wade up, and he hatched the idea. It snowballed from there," he confesses.

"Could you go to jail for it?" I ask concerned for Maddux and Christy by association.

"Attending the underground poker games is illegal," Maddux states. "And stealing from them while there is also illegal."

"But they are breaking the law by attending, too," I seek to further understand.

Maddux nods.

"What charities?" I ask next.

"We split our winnings equally each month, and we each have our own charities we frequent. I donate to Juvenile Diabetes Research Foundation, Wounded Warrior Project, and local Fallen Officer Foundations. The other guys like homeless shelters, foster care, children's hospitals and the like." Maddux's face worries about sharing this knowledge with me.

He's trusting me with... well with his life. I could turn them in; he could go to jail.

"What does that have to do with Willie not being Willie in a courtroom in the past?"

Maddux stares at me, eyes bugged out. Apparently, he thought I knew about the poker games from my vision.

"I'm not sure what you saw Willie doing," Maddux answers. "As far as I know, he's never been arrested. What do you mean 'Willie not being Willie?' Do you mean Witness Protection giving him a new identity?"

Ah-ha! "That may be what I saw. He was signing lots of paperwork and talking about a new life and identity," I share.

"So, you're telling me Willie is his new identity?" I surmise.

"Maybe," I hedge, shaking my head. "I can't be certain."

"You mean I confessed to being a criminal, and you didn't see anything of me and the guys cheating at poker?" he finally asks.

I nod, biting my lips tight.

"Ryan and Christy don't know," he tells me in a whisper.

"I get that. I'm not sure how they might feel about it." I place my hand on his arm. "I get that it's illegal, but everyone there is breaking the law. If they are stupid enough to bet and lose, and you're doing good with their money… I guess no one's getting hurt."

Maddux's head quirks and eyebrows rise at my statement. "Really?"

I nod, smiling.

Maddux hugs me tight to his chest. "I thought I lost you when you touched Willie. I thought I lost you forever."

He will never lose me. I am his for as long as he will have me.

57

I HAVE DIBS

Brooks

*One, Two, Three, Four, Five...*Five golf carts line Ryan and Christy's driveway. *It's a Friday, so it's not ladies' day.* I contemplate turning around. But the girls asked me nicely to run their forgotten iPad to them. I offered to drive over last night, but Christy insisted they endure a night with no screentime, since they left it behind. I know the twins relish their allotted iPad time, so I need to drop it off. *I'll pop in, hand it to Josh, and escape without these golfers seeing me.*

I enter the code in the keypad, letting myself in to Christy's garage. I carefully open the inner door in my attempt to go unnoticed. Josh isn't in the kitchen as I place the iPad on the island.

"Brooks is here!" a dark-haired woman I've not met announces.

Through the open French doors, I star in horror as all attention turns to me.

"What'll it be?" the stranger asks, pouring herself a glass of white wine.

"None for me," I reply. "Thanks. I'm dropping off this..."

"Brookie!" Christy cheers, waving me towards her.

"I'm Sandy," the scantily-clad, dark-haired golfer informs. "Guys make room next to Christy for Brooks."

I reluctantly follow Sandy and her wine.

My best friend pats the empty seat to her right. Scanning the group, I find all have red or white wine.

"We're so glad you could join us," a gorgeous blonde greets. "I'm Paige, I live next to Ryan's brother, Maddux."

Fear floods me. *I wonder if she's spied my car at his house?*

"We'll go around and introduce ourselves," she offers.

"I have a better idea," Sandy announces. "Christy see if you can remember all our names."

Not cool. Talk about putting your host on the spot.

"I've got this," Christy states, sitting on the edge of her seat. "Brooks, on your left is Kirby, she's my age and works at a club downtown."

The tall, slender blonde smiles warmly.

"Beside her, is Gibson, as you can see, she's expecting a baby in June."

Gibson waves sweetly in my direction. I must stare at the red wine glass she holds, because she informs me it's juice.

Christy continues, "Morgan's the red-headed mother of two sons. The tall brunette pacing behind us is Gwynn. You know Josh and you met Sandy and Paige, Maddux's neighbor."

Did she have to mention his name again?

Christy smiles proudly.

"Way to go, Christy!" Sandy cheers.

"So…" I hesitate to ask. "How'd you know my name was Brooks?"

Everyone speaks at once, assuring me Christy didn't talk about me all day.

"Brooks," Gwynn speaks above her friends, demanding my attention. "We all saw *The Back 9 Talk* post with your photo. As Christy's worked with our fundraising committee, she's mentioned her best friend Brooks a few times."

"We're not like some of the old bitties at the club. Any friend of Christy's is a friend of ours," Morgan states.

"I asked about your parlor," Sandy says. "I'm in the market for a tattoo, so I'll be making an appointment."

"Cool." I take in the group. "Which one of you hosts the golf after party on Tuesday with your two hot guy roommates?"

Several women laugh at my phrasing.

"That would be Gibson's condo. And we enjoy the man candy that is Ty while we are there," Gwynn shares.

The pregnant friend speaks up. "That would be me. Ty and Aaron needed the evening off. You must join us sometime."

"So, when Christy offered to host our committee meeting, we jumped at the chance to see her house," Morgan explains.

"So, this," I point to the wine glasses as I speak. "Is a committee meeting?"

"We've conducted our business," Gwynn assures me.

"We decided this year's fundraiser will be a bachelor auction," Morgan informs proudly.

"Let's toast," Sandy urges.

Josh places a glass of white wine in my hand just in the nick of time.

"Too the gorgeous friends on our committee and their genius idea to auction off man candy," Sandy giggles. "I for one, cannot wait to ogle and purchase myself a hottie or two."

"I have dibs on Maddux Harper," Gwynn claims for all to hear.

"Uh-huh," Sandy argues.

"I called dibs first, so he's mine," Gwynn states.

My eyes grow wide. *Bidding on Maddux no way. There's no way he will agree to be auctioned off on stage... A pit forms in my stomach.*

Maddux will participate if approached. He will eat up the female attention. I hope they forget to ask him.

"Uh-oh, I think we scared off Brooks," Gibson tells her friends.

"Ladies," Josh calls for our attention. "Your appetizers are ready inside."

"Ooo... We should have Josh be one of our bachelors," Paige suggests.

Christy and I hang back as the others flock to the food.

"They're a fun bunch," I murmur between sips of wine.

"You don't know the half of it," Christy laughs. "Please say you'll stay and eat with us."

I nod. The closer we get to the doors, the louder they seem.

"He's mine," Sandy bites. "You move on to Justin or Hank."

Gwynn scoffs, "There's no reason we both can't bid on Maddux Harper."

Isn't there any other bachelor for these ladies to fixate on? He's a flashing neon sign in front of my face, demanding not to be ignored.

"Let's settle this on the golf course," Paige suggests.

"Ooo… That's a fabulous idea," Morgan cheers. "Best score? Or a shoot-out?"

The situation causes me to snort. All but Sandy and Gwynn join me in laughter.

"Shoot out," Gwynn demands. "You pick the date."

Sandy stands hands upon her hips, scowl upon her face.

"We could make it a rule that committee members can't bid," Gibson suggests.

"No!" Sandy, Gwynn, Morgan, and Paige argue in unison.

Thirsty much? Seems the women really want to ogle men. Some of them are married. *Drama. Drama. Barack Obama.*

"So… Are there enough bachelors at the club to auction off?" I query.

"We should really write the names down so we can remember them all," Sandy suggests. "Maddux, Justin, and Hank."

"I'm transcribing," Josh informs the ladies his iPad in hand.

Kirby continues to brainstorm, "Ivan, Roy, Derek…"

"Mickey and the elephant in the room…" Gwynn adds with a pause. "Ty."

I hear an audible sigh at the mention of his name. All eyes dart to Gibson. *Perhaps they will focus on Ty instead of Maddux.*

"I'm spit balling here," Paige hedges. "Could we ask one married celebrity to participate to raise even more money?"

I try to follow all eyes as they dart around the group; then I look to my friend. She hasn't processed Paige's statement. I nudge her arm with the stem of my wine glass, lean near her, and whisper, "They're talking about Ryan."

Wide eyes and mouth forming a little 'o', she looks to me.

"It could be fun watching him squirm on stage," I say. "What does he have to do? Go on a date?"

"Nothing that date-like," Paige explains. "They commit to a round of golf and a meal at the club. It's nothing a married member couldn't do."

Eyes pivot to Christy, anxiously awaiting her response.

"I'm sure I could persuade him to volunteer to help," she smiles, with what I am sure is a sexy fantasy playing in her mind.

"Cool. Now we can offer both Harper men as our finale," Paige proclaims.

Once again, the conversation returns to Maddux.

"Ooo-wee!" Sandy cheers. "They'll give me months of spank-bank material."

Christy's right. The ladies are a hoot.

I stick around until the last committee member climbs aboard her cart and sets a course from home.

"I nearly laughed so hard I peed," I admit to Christy and Josh. "Are all committee meetings like this?"

Christy shrugs, "This is my first one, but knowing what I do about the women, I'd say yes."

"I really must meet Aaron and Ty," Josh says. "I can't imagine cooking and serving these women plus up to five more every Tuesday after a round of golf and drinking. They must be saints."

"I have a feeling it's drinking with a side of golf with those ladies," I laugh.

"I've golfed with several of them now," Christy shares. "And I am constantly turning down shots on the course."

"Sounds like Brooks would fit right in," Josh jeers.

I roll my eyes as I smile. The thought of golfing with that group of women doesn't make me nauseous. *I'm not about to volunteer, but if Christy asks me, I will say yes.*

"Look alive ladies," Josh directs. "We have a new rumor post."

While Josh gushes over the blog, Christy has stopped following it, and I follow to be aware of any situations that arise affecting Christy and her family.

Brooks

. . .

The Back 9 Talk—9/29

Everywhere I turn, growing baby bumps are on the rise. There must be something in the water. I don't know about you but I'll be ordering beer only for the foreseeable future.

"Hey," I tap Christy's shoulder with a nearby fork handle at the kitchen counter. "Have something to tell me?"

She turns to face me. "No…" she drawls. "Even if I did, you could simply touch me and find out." She glances at Josh's open iPad

When she gasps, stepping back, hand to her mouth, causing Josh to openly spy on our conversation, I know she figured out why I asked.

"You cow!" Christy scolds. "You're talking about the baby rumor."

I shrug it off. "I though Ryan and you might be eager to add to your brood," I tease.

Josh laughs.

Christy turns to him. "You, too?"

He raises his palms between them.

"You're married adults. I figure as a happily married young couple it won't be long."

Josh shakes his head in agreement.

"Well, nosey people." She points at Josh and me. "Not yet, but it won't be long."

I've seen multiple babies in her future. While I don't have the date, I do know it won't be long.

58

DAMN SEXY

Maddux

In late-October, at Ryan's kitchen island, I fight the urge to strum my fingers on the counter. Emerging from the hallway, Christy finds Josh working at the table while Ryan leans against the kitchen counter and I occupy a stool at the island. She pauses at the entrance to the hallway, admiring Ryan's snug, royal blue button-down.

Josh clears his throat, looking at her. Ryan turns his head to Josh then follow his line of sight. I smile appreciatively. Ryan's eyes bulge...

Ryan prowls towards his wife as she remains frozen in place. Christy is a deer in the headlights, not sure how to react. His mouth encases hers. I cannot look away. When Ryan retreats, panting, he rests his forehead against hers.

"You...that dress... You look stunning," he stammers between his heavy breaths. "I am not sure I will keep my hands off you tonight."

Christy takes a step back, tapping her index finger to the tip of his nose. "Well, you'd better try, or your publicist will find lots of photos and posts to clean up tomorrow."

Ryan shakes his head, leaning his left hand on the corner of the wall. "You are going to be the death of me."

Christy looks into her phone's camera as she applies lip gloss.

"But you will die a very happy man," I chime in.

Eyes still on Christy, Ryan replies, "A *very* happy man."

She swats his hard chest as she walks past him.

"Mom made me promise to send her a pic before we leave," I inform. "I told her there would be photos taken at the club, but she wants one from here."

Christy poses next to Ryan, her side pressing to his. I take two photos before I prompt them to move closer together. They turn, facing each other, her soft curves tight to his hard muscles.

I long to feel Brooks pressed to me, posing for a photo.

"Maddux, please send me the photos," Josh requests. "I will post one or two to Christy's social media."

Josh winks at her. His duties in running Ryan's household grew to helping Christy keep up with her posts.

"The car is here," Josh announces after reading an alert on his iPad. "You kids go have fun. I will want all the details in the morning."

Ryan's driver parks our SUV in front of Ink, Inc in downtown Liberty 15 minutes before we planned to pick up Brooks.

"I will text her to let her know she can come down as soon as she is ready," Christy states.

"Let me tell her," I suggest from my third-row seat. "I need to use her restroom."

Ryan and Christy turn around to peer at me.

"What?" I smirk. "She will let me use her restroom, won't she?"

Christy nods, her eyebrows arch near her hairline and mouth falls agape.

Ryan opens the door and I make my way to Brooks's apartment door.

Ryan and Christy were so caught up in their conversation, they did not notice Brooks and I approaching.

"Let's go," I encourage when all doors are closed.

Movement restricted in her seat; Christy turns as best she can to see Brooks in her spaghetti-strap, little black dress with a tight bodice and flowing skirt. The front falls to mid-thigh. The straps turn in to black angel wings in the back. They are small and beautiful lying flat to her tattooed back. Not wearing her signature fishnet tights, she opted for bare legs between her hemline and treaded, platform, combat boots that nearly reach her knees. Her vibrant leg tattoos contrast with her black attire.

"You look fabulous," Christy tells her friend.

"Fabulous? I said she looks damn sexy," I share.

Ryan's wide eyes find Christy's as she bites her lip to keep from smirking.

When the SUV pulls to the front of the club, the valet opens our passenger side rear door. Christy takes a deep breath in preparation before climbing from the vehicle. She stands awkwardly, waiting on her husband to join her.

"Ready?" Ryan asks, lips near her ear, then kisses her temple.

"Ryan! Ryan!" fans call.

Christy forces a smile upon her face and wraps her arm through his. To say she's nervous would be an understatement. It seems every outing becomes a big production. Ryan's celebrity status draws a lot of attention, and she prefers to blend in rather than stand out. Add to that the fact she has never ventured to a nightclub, and Christy is truly a fish out of water. She turned 21 this year, and she focused on the twins rather than going out with friends. She never partied much. She only knows what to expect from what she's watched on TV and in movies or asked us in preparation for tonight.

"Relax," Ryan coaxes, patting her forearm. He speaks through his smile. "Cameras out here then we get to relax and chill."

"Ryan! Ryan!" fans call from both sides of the ropes.

My brother halts, waving in one direction and then the other. Although he declines requests for selfies and autographs, his fans seem okay with it.

"Tonight, all my attention is on my wife." He grins, and the fans eat it up.

"Thank you." Ryan waves to the crowd before escorting his wife past the line of people waiting to enter the club.

Strobe lights flicker around the upper and lower dance floors while spotlights highlight the bar areas when we enter the club.

Ryan's publicist greets us, ushering us to the right side of the room. A bouncer the size of Ryan's linemen in full pads opens the velvet rope, and we are led up a dimly lit staircase to the less-public second level.

Brooks

The space overlooks the two main dance floors and three bars on the first floor. Christy looks over the glass railing at the crowd below, when I nudge her shoulder.

"You okay?" I ask as we take in our surroundings.

Christy nods.

"Nervous?"

"Yes," she answers. "This world is nothing like our apartment life with the twins."

Ryan's large palm presses into her lower back. "Ladies, our booth is ready."

Maddux follows Ryan's publicist, Mel, and we follow him. Our booth is actually a large, round red sofa with a short round table in the center. The area is dim compared to the brighter lights downstairs. This allows the VIPs more privacy from the general public.

Mel leads the owner over. Ryan rises to greet him and introduces him to Christy, Maddux, and me. Having spent my entire life in the KC area, I know he is part owner of the professional baseball and soccer teams in town, in addition to his family owning vast amounts of real estate across the metro. The two make small talk for a minute while Christy fidgets in her seat beside me.

Returning, Ryan stretches out his arm on the sofa behind her. His hand on her shoulder, he pulls Christy closer to him.

"Oh, my gosh!" our waitress squeals.

"Hey," Christy greets. "I didn't know you worked here. I mean, you told me you worked at a club downtown, but I never thought it might be this one," she rambles.

"You know her?" I ask over the music.

Kirby looks toward me and Maddux at Christy's side. "My name is Kirby, and I will be your bottle girl this evening."

"Kirby is a member at the club," Christy informs the group. "She frequents the pool."

"She's on your golf committee," I recall.

Kirby's smile lights up her face. She is gorgeous. *I bet she makes great tips.*

"I brought bottles of water and glasses of ice for you now," she informs as she places them on the table in front of each of us. "Would you like a beverage menu?" She looks from Maddux to Ryan.

"1492," Ryan says, looking to Maddux for confirmation. Maddux nods.

"And for the ladies, Ciroc Peach," he requests.

Kirby returns with the two bottles Ryan ordered and glasses. She pours our first drinks.

Maddux leans towards me. "Have you been her before?"

I nod, unsure he can hear me above the beats, thrumming around us.

I raise my glass, asking, "Whose turn is it to toast?"

Maddux does not wait for an answer. "Here's to family, friends, bye weeks, and a record-setting football season."

We clink our glasses, and Christy watches the rest of us drink before she takes a tentative sip.

"Like it?" Ryan asks, and she nods.

"I've had it a couple of times before," I admit, listening in on their conversation.

Ryan smiles, proud of his choice. Maddux speaks near my ear, I nod, and he moves to sit on the opposite side of Ryan. Christy moves a little closer to me, making it easier for us to chat for several minutes. I do my best to keep Christy calm in her new environment.

We talk until two women in tiny swaths of black fabric walk past the two of us to approach the guys. I nudge Christy's ribs with my elbow. I'm sure she prays I keep my cool. I can be a spit fire and protect those dear to me.

"Ryan, can we get a photo with you?" the busty redhead asks.

"Ladies, like I told the fans out front, I am keeping all my attention on my wife and guests tonight," Ryan states.

"C'mon," Red urges, crossing her arms under her breasts, further accentuating them. "We're here with…"

"You take the brunette; I get the redhead," I growl in Christy's ear, drawing her attention.

We watch Ryan rise to his feet, preparing to scoot past his brother.

"Your friend should join us, too," the brunette encourages, hopeful.

Of course, Maddux jumps at the opportunity. He positions himself between the women, his arms slinking around both their waists.

"Ryan in the middle with…" the redhead coos.

"I am his brother, Maddux."

The women seem to be enamored with both men. While one presses tightly to Ryan's side, the other does the same to Maddux. Several long seconds pass before the women realize they have no one to take a photo for them.

"Be a dear and take our photo," the redhead says, waving her cell phone toward us.

"I am gonna shove that phone…" I grumble as I rise.

Christy grabs my arm, halting my progress, "Be nice. Cameras will be recording Ryan from everywhere."

I roll my eyes at her. My lips move the entire time I take the pictures.

"All done!" I announce louder than I need to.

To Ryan's credit, he quickly peels the woman from him and returns to Christy. Maddux struggles, but I come to his rescue.

"Honey, I need another drink," I pretend to whine, pulling on his hand.

Hoping for an invitation to join our group, the ladies stand before us, admiring the photo on their phone.

Kirby returns to our table, refilling glasses and replacing empty water bottles while chatting a bit. Before she leaves, she discreetly tilts her head toward the women. Ryan shakes his head. A moment after Kirby disappears, the bouncer ushers the women away from our table.

I lean tight to Maddux's side, leaving no doubt he's not available tonight. His large blue eyes look down at me appreciatively.

"Jealousy suits you," he muses before dropping a bomb. "I'm tired of sneaking around."

My body grows tight at his words.

"Soon. Very soon, I plan to tell Ryan and Christy exactly how I feel about you."

I lick my lips before speaking. "Perhaps you should tell me how you feel about me first," I challenge.

59

JUST A DRESS

Brooks

I did not think this through. My dress is not convenient for the unseasonably cold night we have

"I still can't believe Brooks volunteered to attend tonight," Ryan says from his walk-in closet.

"Well, believe it buddy," I call from the safety of the master bedroom. I don't dare enter the bathroom, in case Ryan is dressing in his attached closet.

"Hey," Christy smiles from the vanity. "Twirl," she orders.

I slowly spin to the right, arms extended, allowing her to see my party dress and heels. Rather than my typical blacks and plaids, I chose a red cocktail dress and heels to fit in tonight. Well, I will fit in as best I can with my many tattoos visible.

"Brooks, you are gorgeous," Christy raves. "Red is definitely your color."

"Red?" Ryan questions from the other room. "Did you say red?"

"Yes, be nice," Christy chides. "You've got to see this."

"I've got one more curl," she informs, returning her gaze to the mirror in front of her. "Wait until the bachelors lay eyes on you." She giggles. "Ryan will have to beat them off with a stick."

"Maybe she won't want me to…" Ryan freezes in the doorway, wide eyes glued on me.

"Whoa," he marvels. "Brooks…you're…holy cow."

"Stop," I beg. "It's just a dress."

"Let me see," Maddux urges, startling me from behind, his arm leaning on the door frame.

When did he get here? I force myself to breath. *He's F-I-N-E in his tux. No way he rented that or bought it off the rack.* It's tailored and hugs every part of him. *Yum, Yum.*

I do not spin, but stand with my hands on my hips as he appraises me. I don't like to admit that I chose this dress to impress him tonight. I wanted him to see that I can fit in at Lynks at Tryst Falls Country Club when I want to.

"Perhaps that's just a dress on the rack. On you, it's…" Maddux searches for words.

My skin heats under his assessing gaze. My body comes to life in his presence. Every part of me hopes for a chance alone with him tonight. I can't get enough of the sensations he elicits in me.

Maddux

Walking down the hall, I hear my brother's voice. He's not talking to Christy. Josh is in the kitchen and the girls are at my parents' house for the night. *Who could he be talking to?*

"Whoa," Ryan marvels. "Brooks…you're…holy cow."

It's Brooks! I lean my forearm on the door frame at the entrance to the master suite. I need the wood to hold me up. I can't believe my eyes. Her black hair is down in long, soft curls. I long to wrap them around my finger. I imagine fisting my hand in her hair while I...*Crap! This may be a long night.*

"Stop," Brooks begs. "It's just a dress."

I've only just arrived, and I can already see it is much more than simply a dress.

"Let me see," I urge, announcing my arrival.

Brooks head jerks in my direction. Her eyes are wide, and her mouth falls open at the sight of me. I'm not sure why she seems so surprised. She was present as Ryan, Christy, and I discussed the charity auction tonight and my invitation to participate. I, on the other hand, was given no hint that Brooks would be in attendance. She is not a member and will not be one of the bachelors auctioned off in the live event. A tiny part of me wonders if jealousy is the reason she decided to tag along.

I take her in. *The red cocktail dress is... Well, it's normal, and Brooks does not wear normal attire. Especially not normal attire for the country club scene. The little red number is sexy and tasteful at the same time. If I have my way, I'll help her slip out of it later.* I fight the urge to adjust my crotch. I anticipated beautiful women gathered around me this evening; I wasn't prepared for the warring emotions I experience in Brooks's presence. *This will be a long, long night.*

I stand up, taking two steps into the room. Within five feet of the breathtaking Brooks, I halt. "On anyone else, it's just a dress," I agree then argue. "On you it's a masterpiece. You are gorgeous." *And I can't wait to tear the fabric off with my teeth, I think to myself.*

"Ahh," Christy melts. "Maddux that was so sweet."

She wouldn't say that if she knew the fantasies the dress evokes within me. I'm slowly coming to understand that I may never work Brooks out of my system, and a small part of me likes the idea of us as a couple.

"We should leave soon. We can't have the man of the night arrive late," Christy teases.

I lean towards Brooks as we exit the bedroom. "Try not to bid on me tonight."

"I brought $200 cash," she states. "I figure that's enough to make me your high bidder."

"Ha, ha," I scoff. "Try not to get jealous when you lose."

"Ryan says I can't bid on you either," Christy pretends to whine.

I wasn't aware she could hear us.

"You're a big boy. I'm sure you can handle whatever desperate housewife wins you tonight," Brooks jests, patting my bicep. "I hope you have your most recent STD test in your wallet for her sake."

"Behave," Christy chides her friend. "It could be one of my new golfing gals that wins Maddux."

Talk about thirsty. I've met the ladies in her golf group and more than one of them scares me.

Brooks

For the umpteenth time I fight the urge to roll my eyes. This event is over the top. Most of the women are married, yet they giggle and chatter about the upcoming male auction like high school girls. As Christy mingles with her friends and other members, she keeps me close to her side. *The event is slated to begin in half an hour; I need to find a moment to slip away.*

"I'm going to the restroom," I speak low near her ear. "I'll be right back."

"I'll go with you," she offers.

I wave my hand in her direction. "I can handle it. Meet you back her in five minutes."

She nods, and I make my escape. I maneuver my way through the attendees standing near cocktail tables and conversing in small groups. At the back of the room, I approach the information table.

"Who do I speak to about making an anonymous bid during the live auction?" I keep my voice low.

"I'm in charge of that. How can I help you?" a jolly older woman answers.

I quickly look over my shoulder to ensure Christy, Ryan, and Maddux are out of sight. "Is there someplace we could talk in private?"

She rises from her chair, motioning for me to follow her. I glance over my shoulder once more, ensuring I haven't been spotted.

Alone in a nearby office, she closes the door. "Now, how can I help you?"

"I'd like to bid anonymously for one of your guys tonight," I explain, fidgeting nervously with the wristband provided for the open bar this evening. "You see, he's a friend, and I don't want him to know I am bidding."

"Okay," she smiles. "Which fella are we talking about?"

"Maddux Harper," I state.

"How much are you willing to spend?" She pulls a notebook from her pantsuit pocket to take down a note. "If you give me your top figure, I can make smaller bids up to but not over that number."

60

ANONYMOUS BIDDER

Maddux

"Ladies and gentlemen," Christy's friend, Robin says into the microphone. "We've come to the final two men in our auction this evening."

The room erupts with cheers and clapping.

"Now our next male is married," she pauses and the women in the crowd boo and hiss. "I know. I know. He's not only a Cardinals NFL superstar, he's a father of adorable twin daughters Harper and Ry, he's married to Christy, and he gives back to our community. Get your paddles ready and bid often for Ryan Harper!"

My brother waltzes onto the stage amid the cat calls, whistles, and cheers. The auctioneer begins his chanting for bids, and I pray the fact that Ryan is married allows my winning bid to be higher than his. *I'll never live it down if he goes for more than I do tonight.*

I look into the crowd, searching for Christy. Not finding her, I scan for Brooks's red dress. *There she is.* Her gaze darts from mine when I catch her looking in my direction. *I really don't want her here for this.*

"Going once. Going twice. Sold for 15-thousand dollars!" the auctioneer announces. "I confirmed that's a new auction record!"

15-thousand. 15-thousand. I need to go for more than 15-thousand.

"Good luck beating that," Ryan taunts, bumping his shoulder into mine on the way past me.

I love my baby brother, but there are times I just want to…

"Maddux Harper!" Robin introduces, signaling my cue to cross the stage.

I strut forward, wearing the smile that works on all the women. I pause in the center of the stage, raising my chin, then blowing a kiss to the crowd. The females go wild. *15-thousand here I come.*

"Paddles up and let the bidding begin!" Robin claps, after handing the microphone to the auctioneer.

I try desperately to understand the auctioneer's mumbo jumbo, but I can only make out every six or seventh word. I chance a glance toward Christy and Brooks, finding Ryan has returned to Christy's side. He holds two paddles in his hands, pretending to slowly raise them to his shoulders then dropping them down. *I better beat him.*

Brooks waves her fingers slightly, careful no one witnesses it. Christy smiles widely, giving me a thumbs up as encouragement.

I bring my attention back to the auctioneer. *Did he just say? Wait! He did! He said 10-thousand. The bids seem slow.* My mind scrambles for something I can do to spur the women to bid.

I spin dramatically, glancing playfully over my shoulder to the crowd. I lower the left shoulder of my tux jacket off my shoulder, as if it exposes bare skin. The crowd cheers, fueling me on. I remove one arm then the other, hanging my jacket from my index finger over my shoulder. I walk toward the left side of the stage and then slowly towards the right.

My antics seem to be working. Often more than one paddle attempts to bid at the same time. Next, I remove my bow tie and unbutton my shirt, baring my chest. Wanting more, the crowd cheers as they bid. I remove my cufflinks, tucking them carefully into my pants pocket, then remove my shirt. I contemplate tossing it into the crowd, remember what I paid for it, and decide to place it on the podium beside me.

"More! More! More!" the women chant.

I shake my finger at them. I turn my back to the crowd and swivel my hips for their amusement, while I fasten my bowtie around my neck. I spin around, continuing to swivel my hips suggestively, remaining PG-13 for the older female members. *I wouldn't want to cause a heart attack. It is a charity auction after all.*

"Going once. Going twice. Sold!"

I strain to hear the amount of the winning bid.

"We have yet another record bid!" Robin cheers. "Let's hear it for the Harper brothers!"

As the crowd applauds the success of the fundraiser, I gather my shirt and jacket, scurrying to exit the stage.

"Dude, who was the winning bidder?" My neighbor, Bill asks, as he pats me on the back.

"I kept trying to see the lady, but she must have been way in the back," Brock adds.

Several of my golfing buddies congratulate me and tease me about the bidder being a sixty-five-year-old member. I take their teasing, all the while my eyes scanning the room for my family and Brooks.

"Excuse me." I wave at the guys and make my way further into the crowd.

Red. Red. Red.

There. Her back is turned towards me, but I'd know that body anywhere. Ryan lifts his chin in greeting as I approach.

"Wow!" Christy wraps me in a tight hug.

"Congrats," Ryan smiles.

"You sure put on quite a show," Brooks accuses.

"I had to make sure I made more money than my little brother," I explain. I didn't think about how my exposition would look to her. "It's for a good cause."

"Suddenly, interested in homeless shelters?" Brooks challenges.

I reach my hand for hers, stopping myself before Ryan or Christy see the motion.

"I wanted to make my sister-in-law look good. She's a member of the ladies golf league hosting this event," I inform Brooks what she already knows.

"Whatever," Brooks mumbles.

Is she jealous, or is this an act for Christy and Ryan's benefit? I decide to tread lightly as I can't quite read her.

"Where is the lucky woman that bid on you?" Ryan asks.

"I couldn't see her from the stage. I wonder who made such a large donation for the opportunity to golf and share a dinner with me?"

"That's an obscene amount of money to play golf with you," Brooks spits.

"It includes dinner, too," I remind her.

"I need to pee," she tells Christy. "Come with me."

The women head in the direction of the restroom, and Ryan moves to my side.

"See the lady in the white pantsuit with the feather in her hair?" he motions to the back of the room.

"Please tell me she isn't the woman that bid on me," I groan, taking in the older, rotund women.

That would be just my luck. I earned more than Ryan but am saddled with her for a day of golf and dinner.

"She didn't bid with a paddle, but she signaled the auctioneer, and he increased the bids," he informs. "You should go ask her who the winning bidder is. I think she's in charge of this entire event."

My feet are frozen in place. I'm curious about the bidder, but fear causes me to pause.

"C'mon," Ryan nudges me. "I'll go with you."

I shuffle my feet, moving slowly in her direction.

"Hello," she greets as we approach. "You gentlemen raised a lot of money this evening."

"Happy to do our part," Ryan assures her. "We were wondering who the winners were."

"Winners?" she asks.

"The bidders," I explain.

"Here you go," she passes an envelope to each of us.

I stare at the white envelope in my hand with my first and last name typed upon it. *Inside will be the name of the winning bidder. It's only a round of golf and dinner,* I remind myself. *I raised more money than Ryan, it doesn't matter what the bidder looks like.*

Christy and Brooks return before I peek inside. I tuck the envelope in my jacket pocket. *My fate can wait.*

"Shall we go?" Ryan suggests.

The envelope in my pocket weighs me down. It's too dark in the SUV to sneak a peek at it. *I'll wait until I return home.*

Brooks slides her hand against the outside of my thigh. Looking her way, I notice her hand is in the dark. I place my hand on hers. Electricity flows up my arm at the contact. I feel like a fifteen-year-old sneaking to hold my girlfriend's hand in the back seat of my parents' car. I release her hand, pulling mine back in my lap as we approach the gate. With extra streetlights in that area, I can't be sure we won't be seen.

Ryan presses the overhead button, and the heavy iron gates part for us.

"Come in for a drink before the two of you head home," Ryan suggests with a glance in the rearview mirror.

I look toward Brooks. When she nods, I decide to ask her to come to my place instead of driving home this evening. We climb from the vehicle, following Christy into the house. She pauses at the kitchen island.

"I can't take it another minute," she announces. "Who bid on you?"

"I haven't looked," I confess.

"No time like the present," Ryan urges.

Brooks hand darts in front of me, snagging the envelope from the pocket of my coat. I try to stop her, but she is too quick. I watch with anticipation and horror as she pulls a card from the envelope.

"Anonymous!" Christy reads out loud. "Anonymous? How can the bidder be anonymous? I mean you need to know who she is in order to golf and dine with her."

"This is too funny," Brooks states. "Have fun golfing with your anonymous lady friend," she calls over her shoulder as she pulls a water bottle from the refrigerator.

She's enjoying this mystery. *She's enjoying it too much.*

Wait until I get her alone.

61

BUSTED

Maddux

I pace the hallway, waiting on Brooks to emerge from the bathroom. I strategically waited two minutes after she excused herself before I pretended I planned to peek in on the twins in their playroom. I hoped to sneak in a moment alone with her.

Brooks startles when she opens the door to find me hovering. "Oh, hey," she says.

I do not speak; I act. I paste my mouth to hers. My hands slide down her ribs to grasp her hips. I pull her tighter to me. I need...

"They're kissing! Mommy! Uncle Maddux and Miss Brooks are kissing!" Harper yells.

Noooo.

"Frickety. Frick. Frick. Frack." Brooks hisses.

"Umm," Ry points at her. "You said a naughty word. Four times."

"Mommy, Miss Brooks said the F-word," Harper tattles yet again.

Brooks eyes implore me to make this entire scene disappear. If I could rewind and not meet her in the hallway, I would. I cannot take the fear on Brooks's face; I would do anything to make it go away.

"Ry and Harper, Mr. Josh wants your help making Daddy's smoothie," Christy tells her daughters to remove them from the hallway.

Her eyes burn like lasers upon my face. She hates me. Clearly, she thinks I pounced on her best friend. I want to tell her this didn't just happen—that I am not taking advantage of her friend, but I don't.

"This," Christy points at me then to Brooks and back. "Whatever this is…"

"Stop!" Brooks interjects.

Christy and Ryan's eyes grow wide as saucers.

"He didn't just kiss me," Brooks bites. "This isn't new. This isn't what you think it is. We're…We've…"

"We've been secretly seeing each other since your wedding," I defend, coming to Brooks's rescue.

I don't look to her. I don't want to see her anger that I am defending her.

"We're not stupid," I continue. "We didn't have a one-night stand and mess up all of this." I swirl my fingers between the four of us. "We, Brooks and I, didn't want to jeopardize anything. We've been sneaking around for three months to make sure we wouldn't hurt the two of you or the twins. We know what's at stake here. We fought this." I point between Brooks and me. "We fought this. We avoided each other. We tried to make it a one-night thing. We tried to make it a week thing. I love her. I love Brooks, and I pray to god she loves me, too. I'm tired of sneaking, I'm tired of hiding how I feel, and I'm telling you now that I plan to spend the rest of my life proving it to her."

I take Brooks's hand in mine, intertwining our fingers, while looking at her with pride. She squeezes it in solidarity.

Christy's narrowed eyes move to her friend.

"We didn't keep our secret to hurt you," Brooks tells her friend. "We kept it a secret to make sure we were… we are…"

"We needed to make sure we were more than friends with benefits before we shared," I explain. "We are in love, we are seeing each other, and we don't need your blessing, but we hope to have it."

"Daddy, is Uncle Maddux in trouble?" Ry asks, concern upon her face.

"No, sweetheart," Christy answers, turning to her daughter. "Uncle

Maddux didn't tell Mommy and Daddy something, so now he needs to explain. While we have our adult conversation you and your sister help Mr. Josh in the kitchen."

Harper nods before jogging back toward the kitchen.

"You," Christy points at Brooks. "With me. Now." She turns on her heel, marching towards the master bedroom.

"I guess we will...talk on the deck," Ryan chuckles.

"Dude," Ryan calls for my attention. "You made a good choice with Brooks."

That is not the reaction I anticipated.

"She'll make great football breeding stock," he claims.

"Oh my god, bro. Do not let Brooks hear you say that," I laugh. "She will rip you limb from limb."

Ryan laughs with me. "Christy would, too."

He is right. Christy would kill him, and Brooks's genes will make adorable, athletic children. In my mind I watch a boy and girl play catch in my back yard. Several scenarios rapidly play out. All of them include Brooks and I with future children. Surprisingly, the thought of marrying Brooks doesn't scare me. It seems natural.

I love Brooks.

Now the big question is if she loves me back?

Brooks

Christy's stare from across the bedroom weighs heavy on me. I fidget as if she's my mother, lecturing me on my behavior during Sunday mass.

"Why didn't you tell me?" Christy inquires. "I thought we told each other everything. I thought we trusted each other. I..."

"Christy, I... we..." I lift my arms exasperated. "I do trust you, I do tell you almost everything, I don't share my visions with you, and I didn't tell you when Maddux and I first hooked up because you were on your honeymoon, and I..."

"My honeymoon?" Christy screeches. "The two of you hooked up on my honeymoon?"

I blush.

"While the girls were in the next room?"

I didn't know her voice could screech that high.

"While your family enjoyed your beach day," I assure her.

"The CVS condoms were for you!" she ascertains correctly. "I'm such an idiot."

"You are not an idiot. Maddux and I were very careful to keep it from you," I state.

"So, this thing between Maddux and you is real; you have feelings for him and it is not just sex?" She seeks further assurance. "And you are in love?"

"Real-yes. Feelings-yes. Love..." I drawl. "We never..." I pause, overcome by emotion. "We never said we love each other before..."

"Today," Christy finishes for me, and I nod.

"He said he loves me, right?" I think aloud. "I didn't imagine that. Maddux declared he loved me in front of Ryan and you, right?"

Christy sucks her lower lip between her teeth, her eyes glisten with happy tears, and she nods emphatically. "My brother-in-law is in love with my best friend." She claps as she hops in place. Suddenly she freezes. "Wait! You love him, right?"

"I think I do," I giggle.

"Think?" Christy balks.

"I love him," I state. "I'm in love with Maddux."

There. I said it out loud. Granted Maddux was not in the room, but admitting it is the first step.

"I'm in love with Maddux," I state, loudly.

"Yay!" Ry and Harper cheer from the doorway.

I roll my eyes. I've told my best friend and her daughters, but I have not confessed my love to Maddux. He declared his love for me in front of his family, but…"Give me a minute."

I exit the bedroom, I walk down the long hallway, searching the open living space for the men. Josh smiles from the kitchen.

"Where are the guys?" I ask.

He points on the deck.

I walk like a woman on a mission.

"Sorry to interrupt," I state making a bee line for Maddux at the railing beside his brother.

I place my hands on his cheeks, the delicious stubble of his whiskers grind into my palms. I gaze into his blue eyes but a moment before I plaster my lips to his. There is no tongue it is simply lips massaging lips, conveying openly in front of Ryan my feeling for this man. Gasping for breath, I pull away. Maddux rests his forehead to mine.

"I love you, too," I murmur.

"About damn time!" Ryan cheers.

"What Daddy?" Ry asks her father.

"Uncle Maddux and Miss Brooks are dating," he explains to the twins.

Ry wraps her arms around Maddux and my legs for a hug while Harper cheers.

"Maddux and Brooks sitting in a tree. K-i-s-s-i-n-g. First comes love, then comes marriage, then comes a baby in a baby carriage," the twins sing.

"Our public-school education dollars at work," Ryan grumbles.

Christy swats him.

"Kiss! Kiss! Kiss!" the twins chant.

I cross my arms across my chest and roll my eyes at their antics.

Maddux leans towards me, placing a chaste kiss upon my cheek. This causes the girls to cheer and clap again.

"No more sneaking around," Maddux murmurs in my ear.

Part of me will miss the intrigue of keeping our secret.

Brooks

Brooks

A large yawn overtakes me. I glance at the clock; it's nearing eleven. My first appointment tomorrow is at noon, but I have some accounting tasks I need to take care of before that. *I should leave soon.*

"Brooks, we should head out. The newlyweds need to put the kids to bed so they have the house to themselves; they don't need us in the way," Maddux pretends to murmur loud enough for Christy and Ryan to hear.

"Good night," I sing song with a wave as I walk to the garage entrance at the side of the kitchen. "Text me in the morning."

We say our good byes before Maddux opens my car door for me.

"I was kinda hoping you might come by my place," he murmurs low.

His sweet confession and eager face are all it takes to convince me. I nod.

I allow Maddux to back his golf cart out of the driveway while I wave one more time to Christy as she still stands in the garage. Then I pull from the driveway and say a quick prayer that she doesn't watch my headlights until I round the curve. If she does, she will see that I pull into Maddux's driveway. I guess she knows we love each other, so it should come as no surprise.

Maddux parks his golf cart in its assigned spot and opens the larger door for me to pull my car into the garage. *So… he plans on me spending the night. It's not the first time.* He prefers I park inside when I sleep over to avoid the neighborhood and club gossip. I round the front of my car towards Maddux to the slight hum of the garage door closing.

"This dress is…amazing," Maddux says with lustful eyes. "It's been torture to keep my hands off you all night."

"So, you like it," I grin, stepping through the mudroom into his kitchen.

"I love it," he assures. "You wore it on purpose, didn't you?"

I raise an eyebrow.

He traces a finger over my shoulder and down my bare arm, causing goosebumps to prickle my skin. Maddux leans towards me, slowly licking his lips. I wet my lips in anticipation of our kiss. He's not gentle; his lips press feverishly to mine. His kiss is needy and promises pleasure in my future.

62

HUGGING YOU IN SPIRIT

Brooks

Christy and I load our arms full of shopping bags, struggling to carry them into the house. Clearly, we went a bit overboard on holiday shopping today.

"Will you ever allow me to do my job?" Josh huffs when we unload our arms loads on the mudroom bench. "I should have carried those bags in for you."

"Well..." I drawl, smiling. "There are many more where those came from."

Josh shakes his head laughing on his way into the garage.

"Shall we wrap today or hide them?" I ask, hoping we pour drinks and relax the rest of the day.

"I'm afraid we must wrap them immediately," Christy laughs. "Ryan cannot stand not knowing what gifts are. He will search the house high and low to find them all."

"We will make it a wrapping party," Josh announces. "Wine or drinks? What will it be?"

"Wine," we answer in unison, causing the three of us laugh.

Along with the drinks, Josh places multiple pairs of scissors, tape, rolls of wrapping paper, and name tags upon the table and kitchen island. He opens a holiday playlist on his nearby iPad, and we set to work wrapping and labeling the plethora of gifts.

Over an hour passes before we adorn the final three items with festive paper. I reach for the tape without looking. My hand rests upon Christy's. *Visions. I see myself in her future.* I do not remove my hand from hers. For once I allow it to play out before my eyes. Worried for me, Christy pulls her hand from under mine, breaking the connection, ceasing the vision.

"Brooks..." Christy murmurs, her voice heavy with concern. "You had a vision."

It's a question and a statement.

"I was with you in the future," I state, still processing what I saw.

My mouth is dry, and the world spins.

I...I...

I excuse myself to the restroom, needing to escape for a moment. In the mirror above the sink, I find my face pale. I fill my hands with water, splashing it over my eyes and cheeks.

Christy taps lightly on the closed door. "Brooks, may I come in?"

I pat my face dry on a hand towel. "I'll be right out." I take a deep calming breath, that doesn't work, and open the door. I follow my friend back to my stool in the kitchen.

Josh finished our packages; now he scurries about the space returning items to their rightful places.

"Care to talk about it?" Christy offers.

"I... I'm..." I stammer. "I'm not sure. It can't be... I'm unable to..."

She slides my now full wine glass towards me, urging me to take a sip.

"You saw my future and you were in it," she starts for me. "What was I doing?"

My eyes fly to hers.

"It's okay to share, I really want to know this one," she assures.

"But you never want..." I begin to argue, and Josh stops nearby to listen.

"This one seems important," Christy states. "I'm a little intrigued to find out what you were doing in my future."

I shake my head, still unable to fathom it.

"When was it?" she asks.

"I'm not sure when."

"Where was it?" she continues to encourage me to share.

"We were in Hawaii at the Pro Bowl," I shrug, knowing that doesn't really help with the when.

"Were we watching Ryan?" she prods.

I nod my head. "We were at the beach." I look to Josh. "You and Paul were there. You were building a sand castle while the girls surfed with Maddux."

"Okay," Christy smiles. "So, what were we doing?"

I stare at my friend, unsure the next part is possible. "Perhaps I'm coming down with that flu bug everyone passed around at Thanksgiving last week."

"Brooks, what were you and I doing?"

"I was holding...baby," I whisper.

Christy bites her lips as tears of joy well in her eyes.

While I heard her ask me to tell her everything I saw, I leave out the part that she held her new son beside me.

"We're having a baby!" Josh squeals.

Christy swats the air between them, attempting to calm his celebration.

"So, Maddux and you have a baby," she smiles. "This is the best Christmas gift you've ever given me. I now know the two of you will get married and have a baby!"

"How old was the baby? Was it a boy or a girl?" Josh rapidly seeks all the details.

"He was walking in the sand, so..." I try to process what age that might be.

"He! She said he!" Josh claps from the other side of the island.

"If he's walking in sand, I would estimate him to be about two," Christy thinks out loud. "What else happened?"

"He hugged me and tried to sit on my lap," I giggle at the thought. "My belly made it hard for him."

"Oh. My. God!" Christy squeals. "You are pregnant again!"

"Two babies in our future!" Josh cheers, hopping up and down.

"But it's not possible," I argue. "I can't touch. I can't have babies. They'd give me visions. If not in the womb, then when I held them. I can't be a mother…"

"Yes, you can!" Josh scolds. "You saw it in a vision so you can and will be a momma."

I search Christy's face for… I'm not sure what I search for. She doesn't understand my gift any more than I do. *I can't have kids. A mother must touch, she must hold, she must use contact to demonstrate her unconditional love for her children—I can't do that with my visions. Can I?*

"You must have faith," Christy implores. "If you held your son in the vision, then he didn't cause visions. You get to be a mother."

"Of two," Josh adds, his face full of love for me.

It still blows my mind. Because Christy bumped into Ryan again, I gained new friends in Ryan, Josh, and Paul. I smile at my friends.

Christy taps upon her iPhone.

"Don't tell anyone!" I scold.

"I'm not," she assures me. "I know where the next four Pro Bowls are located… so I know when your vision occurs." She smiles smugly.

My eyes grow wide. *She knows the date of my vision in Hawaii. She knows when the scene of me be pregnant with our second child takes place. The shoe is on the other foot, and I'm not sure I like it. This must be akin to how she feels when I have visions of her and the girls. I want to know, but I don't.* I know that Maddux and I will be together for at least three or so years, and we will have two children. It's eerie.

"Well?" Christy smirks, sensing my hesitation.

I pull my lips tight between my teeth as I look to my friend.

"I won't tell you, but I will give you a hint," Christy offers, enjoying my discomfort a bit too much. She hops off her stool, walking quickly down the hallway.

I look to Josh; he smiles and shrugs back at me.

Christy returns, holding her hands behind her back.

"I have a gift for you," she announces, a ginormous smile upon her face. Her eyes dance with excitement. "You can cancel your appointment next week with my gynecologist, and you probably need this."

I reach for the white and pink box she extends towards me. As I pull it toward me, I make out the words upon it. My eyes grow wide and my cheeks heat. *Josh!* I hide the box under the counter, shooting daggers at my friend.

Christy laughs at my discomfort. I decide to get even with her. I pass the box back, shaking my head at her as I tisk.

"You'll need this one, I'll buy my own," I state, loving her shock.

"Your vision?" she asks, already knowing the answer before I nod. "Together?" she says through her tears of joy, and again I nod.

"Umm... hello," Josh scorns. "Stop talking in code and fill me in."

Through our tears, Christy and I giggle. She slides the pregnancy test across the kitchen island in his direction. He clutches his chest as he rounds the counter to hug Christy.

"Brooks, I'm hugging you in spirit," he proclaims, his arms around my friend. "My two favorite girls are having babies!"

The End

I hope you will look for future stories in *The Lynks at Tryst Falls Series* of stand-alone books releasing in 2023.

Help readers find this story and give me a giant author hug--please consider leaving a review on Amazon, Goodreads, and BookBub—a few words mean so much.

Look at my Pinterest Boards for my inspirations for characters and settings. (Link on following pages.)

ALSO BY BROOKLYN BAILEY:

Lynks at Tryst Falls Series-
Gibson -- #1

Christy -- #2

Ali's Fight

Country Roads Series-
Memory Lane

Dusty Trail to Nowhere

Fork in the Road

Take Me Home

The 7 Cardinal Sins Series-
Bend Don't Break

Behind the Locked Door

Starting Over

Whatever It Takes

Chance Encounter

Trivia Page

1. Character names in this book are those of famous MLB Baseball players.
2. Tryst Falls is a natural waterfall located in Excelsior Springs, Missouri to the north and east of Kansas City. Its name came about as young couples often met and picnicked here. I dare say it has witnessed a tryst or two.
3. Kansas City is in Missouri-well, most parts that you think/hear of are. (KCI Airport, the Chiefs at Arrowhead, the Royals at Kauffman, Worlds of Fun, the Power & Light District, & zoo are all in Missouri) I've attended many concerts where the lead singer says something along the lines of "Kansas how are you tonight?" when the concert is held in Missouri.

ABOUT THE AUTHOR

Brooklyn Bailey's writing is another bucket-list item coming to fruition, just like meeting Stephen Tyler, Ozzie Smith, and skydiving. As she continues to write sweet romance and young adult books, she also writes steamy contemporary romance books under the name Haley Rhoades, as well as children's books under the name Gretchen Stephens. She plans to complete her remaining bucket-list items, including ghost-hunting, storm-chasing, and bungee jumping. She is a Netflix-binging, Converse-wearing, avidly-reading, traveling geek.

A team player, Brooklyn thrived as her spouse's career moved the family of four, fifteen times to four states. One move occurred eleven days after a C-section. Now with two adult sons and a grandson, Brooklyn copes with her newly emptied nest by writing and spoiling Nala, her Pomsky. A fly on the wall might laugh as she talks aloud to her fur-baby all day long.

Brooklyn's under five-foot, fun-size stature houses a full-size attitude. Her uber-competitiveness in all things entertains, frustrates, and challenges family and friends. Not one to shy away from a dare, she faces the consequences of a lost bet no matter the humiliation. Her fierce loyalty extends from family, to friends, to sports teams.

Brooklyn's guilty pleasures are Lifetime and Hallmark movies. Her other loves include all things peanut butter, *Star Wars*, mathematics, and travel. Past day jobs vary tremendously from a radio station DJ, to an elementary special-education para-professional, to a YMCA sports director, to a retail store accounting department, and finally a high school mathematics teacher.

Brooklyn resides with her husband and fur-baby in the Des Moines area. This Missouri-born girl enjoys the diversity the Midwest offers.

Reach out on Facebook, Twitter, Instagram, or her website…she would love to connect with her readers.

Sign up for Brooklyn's newsletter here.

- amazon.com/~/e/B0B57RYXZ2
- goodreads.com/BrooklynBailey
- bookbub.com/authors/brooklyn-bailey
- instagram.com/brooklynbaileyauthor
- tiktok.com/@haleyrhoadesbroklynbaley
- facebook.com/BrooklynBaileyAuthor
- twitter.com/brooklynb_books
- pinterest.com/haleyrhoadesaut
- linkedin.com/in/haleyrhoadesauthor
- youtube.com/@haleyrhoadesbrooklynbaileyauth

Made in the USA
Monee, IL
03 August 2023